"I know why you came here, senhorita."

The Duque's tone was biting. "You didn't really need a job. You came here to escape a man—a millionaire, in fact. Robert Lindsay."

Juliet was startled. How had he found out that she was Robert Lindsay's daughter?

The Duque regarded her pale features with contempt. "Wasn't Lindsay's money enough for you?" he sneered. "What are you planning to trade your charms for now—a title?"

Juliet swayed slightly with shock. He thought—he thought she had been Robert Lindsay's mistress!

"Answer me!" the Duque snapped. His voice lowered as he moved threateningly nearer. "Or I will force the truth from your lips."

ANNE MATHER
is also the author of these
Harlequin Romances

and these

Harlequin Presents

Many of these titles are available at your local bookseller.

For a free catalogue listing all available Harlequin Romances, send your name and address to:

HARLEQUIN READER SERVICE,
1440 South Priest Drive, Tempe, AZ 85281
Canadian address: Stratford, Ontario, Canada N5A 6W2

The Arrogant Duke

by

ANNE MATHER

Harlequin Books

TORONTO • LONDON • LOS ANGELES • AMSTERDAM
SYDNEY • HAMBURG • PARIS • STOCKHOLM • ATHENS • TOKYO

Original hardcover edition published in 1970
by Mills & Boon Limited

ISBN 0-373-01451-1

Harlequin edition published December 1970
Second printing January 1979
Third printing May 1979
Fourth printing August 1979
Fifth printing December 1979
Sixth printing April 1980
Seventh printing July 1981

CHAPTER ONE

ESCAPE! Juliet savoured the word even as she felt a faint pang of self-recrimination. She ought not to be feeling so happy just because she had managed, for the first time in her life, to get the better of her father. Even now, at the thought of his anger when he discovered what she had done, she shivered, and hoped with urgent intensity that he would have time to cool down before he discovered her whereabouts. There was little doubt in her mind that he would find her; in his thorough, painstaking way he would explore every avenue until some small clue gave him the necessary lead. But at least for a time, a few months perhaps, she would have the chance to do what she wanted to do for a change.

She looked through the window of the island-hopping hydroplane, finding relief from her thoughts in the unbelievably beautiful panorama spread out below her. Since they left Bridgetown that morning the whole tapestry of islands and deep, deep blue sea had enchanted her, more now than ever before, and she thought for the umpteenth time that the advertisement in *The Times* which she had answered had been made for her. She knew they were nearing Venterra, the dark-skinned steward had already warned her to fasten her safety belt, and she tried to pick out which island it might be. Surely in so many islands her father would never find her without her assistance.

For Juliet, everything now was a novelty. She had never travelled alone before, there had always been the accompaniment of her father's train of assistants, secretaries and servants, luggage and sporting equipment to attend to. It had been exciting to carry her own bag, to hire her own porter, to stay at a small hotel instead of a luxury club, and to choose her own meal.

Mandy, of course, would have been horrified to think of her ewe-lamb staying alone in even so British an island as Barbados, and it was as well that she believed, as indeed did her father, that she was staying with friends for a couple of days. Mandy, or Miss Jane Manders, to give her her correct name, was the nearest person to a mother that Juliet had ever known. Her own mother had died when she was born, much to her father's anguish, and Juliet supposed that maybe that was why he treated her so possessively, placing her in her mother's shoes. Mandy had been thirty then, just recovering from the grief of her own mother's death, and she had taken care of Juliet at once, lavishing all the love she had on the child. Sometimes, Juliet had wondered why Mandy had never got married, and then again she had speculated as to whether her nurse and companion cherished some vain feelings towards her father. But Robert Lindsay certainly gave her no encouragement, and the arrangement which had begun as a temporary thing had lengthened into more than twenty years, and now Mandy could only be regarded as one of the family. It was Mandy who Juliet disliked deceiving most, but as Miss Manders had, over the years, taken over the reins as housekeeper in the large rambling house in Hampstead which had been the home of the Lindsay family for many many years, Juliet knew that her position in the household would not been in jeopardy because she had left.

Thrusting back these thoughts, she allowed her mind to dwell on the immediate future and recalled with some amusement her interview with a firm of solicitors in London. The advertisement had called for a young woman, of good family, to act as companion to a girl of sixteen, recently orphaned, with some degree of disability, who was at present living with her uncle in Venterra, an island not many miles distant from St. Lucia in the West Indies.

Juliet had thought the advertisement suited her lack of capabilities perfectly. Oh, she had many attributes, she supposed; she was well read, could arrange flowers decoratively, spoke several languages, was used to acting as her father's hostess on occasions of importance, and was well able to deal with the sometimes amorous advances of young men her father had chosen as escorts for her.

But basically, she had had no training to follow a career. Her father had never wanted her to become an intellectual, and so her eager mind had had to content itself with learning from books, and the core of dissatisfaction with her empty way of life had been born.

She might never have been courageous enough to do something about it, however, had not her father decided that it was high time she was thinking of getting married. In his usual overbearing way he had produced three young men for her to choose from, but none of them were the kind of man Juliet wanted to marry. She was looking for no knight in shining armour, no gallant paramour to live in a rosy world of romance for the rest of her days. But she did want a man, not some weak-chinned facsimile, who was quite content to allow her father to provide him with every material need in return for marrying his daughter.

She felt an angry sense of injustice, at the remembrance of it all, and then calmed down as she realized she had done the only thing she could, in the circumstances.

The interview had been amusing, though. She had had to remember that her name was now Rosemary Summers and not Juliet Lindsay, and it had been difficult assuming her new identity for the first time. She felt grateful to Rosemary too. She and Rosemary Summers had attended the same boarding school, although Rosemary's parents were both doctors, and Rosemary had followed in their footsteps and was at present a medical student. She and Juliet had always been close friends, even though Juliet's father had attempted to discourage that friendship. He had not considered the Summers suitable associates for his daughter, but in this Juliet had been adamant and so her friendship with Rosemary had continued. They met often, and shared their experiences, Juliet envying the other girl's freedom and her chance to carve a career for herself.

When Robert Lindsay's campaign turned to the subject of Juliet's marriage, Juliet poured out all her troubles to Rosemary. Rosemary was sympathetic, listening with her calm, intelligent mind, weighing up the situation, as she would weigh up a patient's complaints. Then she had said:

'If I were you, I would get a job, anything, just so long as I had some independence.'

Juliet sighed. 'That's all very well for you to say, Rosemary, but he wouldn't let me do that! Heavens, he'd very likely buy up whoever was employing me, and then give me the sack!'

Rosemary smiled. 'Oh, Juliet,' she said, shaking her head, 'there must be something you can do. Somewhere you could go, where he has no influence!'

'Not in this country,' remarked Juliet gloomily.

'Then out of it,' said Rosemary reasonably.

'But how?'

'I don't know.' Rosemary had lit a cigarette before replying, studying its tip with concentration. 'There are always heaps of jobs available for governesses and nannies which entail travel.'

'But I couldn't be either of them,' exclaimed Juliet. 'I've had no training for a job like that!'

Rosemary had had to agree, so the problem had remained unsolved until Juliet read the advertisement for this job which had appeared in *The Times*. She had rung Rosemary and told her, and over a prolonged lunch break they had discussed the pros and cons.

'You must realize that there'll be heaps of applicants for a position like this,' said Rosemary, dousing some of Juliet's enthusiasm.

'Even so, it is a long way away,' Juliet had answered.

9

'Lots of girls won't want to work so far away from home.'

'Maybe,' said Rosemary doubtfully. 'But what about your father?'

'He wouldn't know anything about it until I'd gone,' said Juliet, with decision. 'If I told him he'd only try to stop me.'

'And don't you think he will anyway?' exclaimed Rosemary. 'It will be the easiest thing in the world for him to trace you there.'

'Oh, yes, I suppose you're right. My passport and booking and everything!' Juliet heaved a sigh.

'Of course.' Rosemary studied her sympathetically. 'Oh, Juliet, I don't know what to say.'

Juliet lifted her shoulders, lighting herself a cigarette. 'What is there to say?' she said moodily. Then, as though mesmerized, an idea caused her to allow the match to burn her fingers. 'Ouch!' she gasped, rubbing the injured finger. 'Rosemary, I *have* had an idea! The perfect solution, in fact. If you're agreeable!'

Rosemary lay back in her seat. 'Go on. What is it?'

'Well,' Juliet ran her tongue over her lips excitedly, 'how about my using your passport?'

Rosemary sat up in astonishment. 'My passport!' she echoed.

Juliet nodded vigorously. 'Yes. Oh yes, Rosemary. It's the perfect solution! You know how alike people have always said we are, same hair, same height, same colouring! Those passport photographs are notoriously terrible. No one studies them in detail.'

'They do,' exclaimed Rosemary indignantly. 'But

maybe so far as the photo is concerned you might get away with it. It isn't a very good likeness of me.'

'You see!' Juliet's eyes were alight. 'Your hair is the same colour as mine, and all I'd have to do is wind mine up in that pleat you wear. We're both quite tall and slim, and our colouring is practically the same.

'Your tan is deeper,' returned Rosemary dryly, 'but then I haven't just spent three weeks in the South of France.'

Juliet sighed, and gave a wry smile. 'You may not believe this, Rosemary, but I'd rather be you than me any day of the week!'

Rosemary looked contrite. 'I know, I know,' she said, feeling sorry for what she had hinted. It was true, Juliet did not consider herself lucky. Compared to Rosemary, Juliet's life was empty. 'It would mean you adopting my identity,' she continued thoughtfully.

Juliet's young face darkened. 'Oh, yes, it would,' she said slowly. 'Damn!'

'Well, that's not insuperable,' replied Rosemary consideringly. 'After all, no one knows your name there, or mine either, for that matter. You could be Rosemary Summers; it's not such an uncommon name.'

Juliet looked at her with wide eyes. 'I really believe you're considering it,' she exclaimed. 'Oh, Rosemary, would you? Would you really?'

Rosemary gave a grimace. 'Well, I don't see how I can refuse,' she replied dryly. 'I'm very fond of you, Juliet, and although we're the same age, I always feel years older than you. I don't want to see you forced mentally, if not exactly physically, into an unhappy marriage. There are too many of them around already, and I know that men like Roger Latimer and Stephen Longdon and that awful Jeremy McVane would bore you stiff!'

Juliet clasped her hands together. 'Do you really think I might get away with it?' she exclaimed.

Rosemary shrugged. 'Well, you've got to get the job first,' she replied practically. 'And quite honestly, with your appearance I doubt whether you'd even be considered!'

Juliet frowned. 'Why?'

'Well, you don't look as though you need a job, for a start, and secondly they're bound to want somebody plain, and ordinary, and not too decorative. After all, the West Indies is quite a place. They won't want their suitable applicant finding herself a husband during the first few weeks she's there.'

Juliet looked thoughtful now: 'Yes, you're right, as usual,' she murmured. 'I'll just have to make myself look very plain, and very ordinary, and if I put my hair up as you wear yours that should add a few years!'

'Gee, thanks!' exclaimed Rosemary dryly, and they both collapsed in giggles.

Remembering all this now, Juliet felt a smile curve her lips. Rosemary had been wonderful, particularly as she was aware, just as acutely as Juliet, that she would be the first person Robert Lindsay would contact when he discovered Juliet had disappeared. She would have to be very astute not to be caught out by a man as determined as Robert Lindsay.

The interview had been rather different from Juliet's imaginings. When she arrived at the offices of Benyon, Forster, Benyon and Benyon, she found only one other applicant waiting for interview. She was a girl of around her own age, who confided to Juliet that the job did not appear to be the sinecure it had first appeared to be.

'This girl we're supposed to be companion to – did you know she was confined to a wheelchair?'

Juliet smoothed the skirt of her dark grey suit over her knees. It seemed far too long after the short styles she was used to wearing, but at least it gave her an added sense of confidence.

'Well,' she replied carefully, 'the advertisement did say that she had some degree of disability.'

'Some degree!' the other girl sniffed. 'I don't call an invalid in a wheelchair only partially disabled! Heavens, I thought maybe she had only one arm or something like that!'

Juliet felt a sense of distaste at the girl's words. 'I don't see that it matters,' she said quietly. 'Surely a girl so young, confined as she is, deserves companionship.'

'It's a nurse they want, not a companion,' retorted the girl shortly. Then she stood up. 'Oh, anyway, I don't think I'll stay. I don't want that kind of a job. It was the locality that appealed to me. Tell them I changed my mind, will you?'

Juliet's eyes widened. 'All right. But are you sure?'

'Of course I'm sure. G'bye. Hope you get it, if you want it!'

After the girl had gone Juliet felt uncomfortable. What would the interviewers think when she had to tell them that one of their applicants had changed her mind? She hoped they wouldn't think she had said anything to deter her.

But when a man who she later discovered to be Mr. Forster came to ask Miss Laurence, as the girl had been called, to come in, and Juliet explained what had happened, he merely shook his head sadly, and said:

'I'm afraid we worded the advertisement wrongly, Miss Summers – it is Miss Summers, isn't it?' and at Juliet's nod: 'All the applicants appear to have believed Miss de Castro had some mild disablement that would not inconvenience themselves too greatly. I gather Miss Laurence advised you of the facts of the matter.'

Juliet rose to her feet. 'Yes, she did.'

He nodded. 'I see. It was very kind of you to wait and see me.' He sighed. 'We must advertise again.'

Juliet drew her brows together. 'Do I take it then that I'm unsuitable?'

Mr. Forster stared at her. 'You mean – you're prepared to take the job?'

Juliet bit her lip. 'Well, yes, if you're prepared to interview me.'

Mr. Forster rubbed his hands together. 'Oh, indeed, yes, indeed, Miss Summers. Come in – come in! I'm sure we can work something out.'

And so they did.

Juliet felt the plane bank slightly, and looked down, feeling the bubble of excitement rising inside her again. What had Mr. Forster said? That the girl, Teresa, had been injured in the same car crash which had killed both her parents; that she was paralysed from the waist down; that the accident had happened six months ago, and since she came out of hospital she had been living on Venterra with her uncle, Felipe de Castro.

They were losing height rapidly now, flying low over the island, giving Juliet a marvellous view of a thickly wooded central area, high peaks emerging above the tops of the trees; a coastline of bays and coves, with the inevitable line of a reef some distance out from the shore; villages nestling at the foot of the hills, fishing boats nudging stone jetties; pastel-painted houses, and the tiles of more sophisticated dwellings, standing in their own grounds. The brilliance of the sun accentuated the greenness of the foliage and the exotic colour of the flowers and trees. She breathed a faint sigh, half relief, half apprehension, for now she had to face her future employer, and her future charge.

She was the only passenger on the hydroplane, apart from Louis, the steward, who had welcomed her aboard. She had gathered from his comments that the plane belonged to Senhor de Castro, her future employer, and was used because there was nowhere smooth and flat enough to support an airstrip. Mr. Forster had told her that Senhor de Castro was a Portuguese gentleman, who had sugar estates on the island,

and that apart from herself his household accommodated several servants, including an American nurse for Teresa. Altogether it sounded quite delightful, and Juliet, enchanted with her own freedom, was revelling in it all.

The hydroplane came down on the smooth surface of a bay, which was edged by a small community of cottages, the boats by the jetty rocking as the plane caused the water to swell considerably. Juliet loosened her seat belt, looked back at Louis, and said:

'We've arrived?'

Louis nodded his head. '*Sim, senhorita,*' he said. 'This is Venterra. You like?'

Juliet smiled. 'Yes, I like. What do we do now?'

Louis stood up and came to her side. 'See, Pedro has already started for the plane with his boat, eh!'

Juliet looked through the window as he pointed, and saw the small rowing boat approaching them. 'Oh, yes. Thank you, Louis.' Then: 'How will I get to the de Castro home?'

Louis unstrapped her suitcases from their position in the rear, and then said: 'Do not worry, *senhorita*. A car will have been sent for you.'

'I see.' Juliet wished she could dispel the apprehension which was rapidly overtaking all other emotions. 'Is it far to the house?'

'The *quinta, senhorita*! No, it is not far. Miguel will take you.'

Juliet decided she had asked enough questions. It would not do to sound too curious about her employers. She wondered if Senhor de Castro was married. It seemed likely, and yet Mr. Forster had not mentioned it. He must be quite old. Mr. Forster had said that Teresa was the daughter of his *younger* brother, and as Teresa was sixteen it did not take a great deal of mathematical skill to work out that this man must be in his forties at the very least. She hoped, feeling a twinge of nervousness assail her, that he was not the kind of man to make passes at his employees. Such an idea had not occurred to her before, and yet now it loomed large and rather disturbing.

The small craft touched the hydroplane, and the pilot threw open the door so that Juliet could emerge and climb into the boat. She had decided to wear a slack suit for the journey, and now she was glad she had. Getting in and out of small rowing boats was not the easiest thing to do while endeavouring to hold down a skirt.

The heat here was tempered by a faint breeze, and the boat rocked gently. The scents of the island, a tang of salt and sea and the perfumes of the flowers, mingled with the sweet smell of the cane, and Juliet took a deep breath, shedding a little of her apprehension.

Pedro, the boatman, was dark-skinned like Louis, but with more European features. He grinned cheerfully at the pilot and Louis, and gave Juliet a speculative glance before taking the cases and stowing them in the bottom of the small boat. After a brief conversation with his compatriots, he again took the oars and rowed rhythmically back to the stone jetty. Juliet was aware that their progress had attracted quite a deal of attention from women and children on the jetty, and she tried to interest herself in her surroundings to exclude her embarrassment. There was certainly plenty to see, the attractively painted cottages jostling each other, the fishing vessels with dark nets stretched out to dry, the palms that encroached almost to the water's edge in places, and most incongruous of all a low-slung cream convertible which was parked on the road which wound between the narrow houses.

Pedro nodded to the automobile. 'Miguel,' he said, by way of an explanation. He pointed to himself. 'Er – Pedro's – brother.'

'Oh yes,' Juliet nodded politely, recalling that Mr. Forster had not said she needed a foreign language here. It would prove awkward if they all spoke mainly Portuguese. Although she knew Spanish, Portuguese was not one of her languages.

They reached the jetty, Pedro threw out the painter, and another man who was very much like Pedro caught it and tied the boat securely to the capstan.

He helped Juliet to climb on to the stone pier, and grinned down at his brother. His gaze turned back to Juliet, his eyes indicative of the appreciation he felt. 'You are Senhorita Summers?'

'Yes,' Juliet nodded again. 'Did Senhor de Castro send you to meet me?'

Miguel's eyes narrowed. 'Er – *sim, senhorita*. I suppose *o Duque* did send me!'

'*O Duque!*' Juliet translated rapidly. The Duke! *What duke?* 'Who – who might the *Duque* be?' she asked slowly.

'O Duque Felipe Ricardo de Castro!' replied Miguel calmly. 'The man who is to be your employer!'

'My employer – is – is a duke? I don't believe it!' Juliet was astounded.

'But I understood from – from the solicitor in London—' She halted again. She was asking too many questions once more. After all, there was a possibility that Mr. Forster had deliberately refrained from telling her that her employer was to be a duke. After the problems he had had hiring someone, maybe he had thought that such a revelation would jeopardize his chances of obtaining a satisfactory applicant.

Miguel was studying her with some amusement in his dark eyes, and Juliet gathered her scattered senses. After all, what of it? She had met dukes before, and they were only people like anyone else. What was there to alarm her?

She compressed her lips 'Is this the car?' she asked, amazed at her own composure.

Miguel inclined his head. *'Sim, senhorita.* Ah, Pedro, have you got all the luggage? Good. Come, *senhorita.'*

She followed Miguel across to the car, ignoring the speculative glances of the group of islanders who watched them with interested dark eyes. Really, thought Juliet, with something like annoyance at her own disturbed frame of mind, what was she getting so het up about? Just because she had discovered that her employer was a Portuguese duke. It was ridiculous!

But still she couldn't banish the thought that a duke

was slightly different from a mere *senhor*, and in her precarious position the fewer complications there were the better.

Miguel stowed the cases, had a good-natured chatter with Pedro, then slid into the front seat of the automobile, and set it in motion. They drove along the quayside, past the now waving children, whose mothers gave wide smiles, and up a curving track which led along the coastline. The steep gradient brought them to a higher road which wound round the heavily foliaged hillside. Here Juliet had a magnificent view of the whole coast, its bays and headlands giving it a wild and untamed beauty. The coves were white with coral sand, rocks rearing their ugly heads above the creaming surf. Inland was the exotic beauty of plant life, bushes of oleander and hibiscus providing brilliant splashes of colour, while some rarer varieties which Juliet could not name added their own pink and gold charm to the view. They were sweeping down again now, into a valley whose walls were networked by fast-flowing tumbling streams, at whose brink tiny blue flowers grew. A river ran through the valley floor and here were fields of waving sugar cane, and the sweet smell was intoxicating.

Unable to resist, she leaned forward, and said: 'Does this plantation belong to – to the Duke?'

Miguel glanced round once, and then returned his attention to the road. '*Senhorita*, this whole island belongs to the Duque.'

'Oh!' Juliet sat back in her seat.

Miguel, encouraged by her question, remarked: 'Do

you think you will like it here, *senhorita?*'

Juliet bit on her bottom lip. 'I – I'm sure I shall,' she said awkwardly. 'Is – is it far now?'

'Not far,' Miguel answered. And then: 'You have come to be a friend for the young *senhorita,* is that right?'

Juliet hesitated. She had no wish to say too much, but his question seemed innocent enough. 'That's right,' she said now, nodding.

'Senhorita Teresa,' murmured Miguel, almost as though he was speaking to himself. 'Yes, it will not be easy.' And with this cryptic comment he said no more.

They left the valley through a narrow pass in the hillside, towering bastions of rock on either side of the narrow road. They emerged on to a plateau, which fell away steeply at the far side to the shoreline at the other side of the island. The sun was growing higher and the heat seemed intense even in the open vehicle. Juliet fumbled in her bag, and slid dark glasses on to her nose, wishing the journey was over.

Now they were descending again, a winding road along terraces cultivated with coffee beans. Nearer sea-level, they branched on to a side road which brought them to tall gates, standing wide, and a drive which led up to the home of the Duque de Castro.

Juliet caught her breath in a gasp when she saw the *quinta* for the first time. Built of mellowed grey brick, it stood on three sides of a central courtyard, but Miguel brought the car round to the front of the building and halted on a gravelled forecourt. Surrounded by trees which provided a backcloth for its almost medieval beauty, with the sun turning its windows into golden tongues of flame, the *quinta* was imposing and impressive, and wholly unlike anything Juliet had even vaguely imagined. Without waiting for Miguel to assist her, she slid out of the car, and stood looking up at the arched portals of its entrance, emblazoned by the crest of the de Castro family. Through an arched hallway, the central courtyard could be seen where a fountain played in its centre, providing a constant and cooling sound of running water.

Miguel smiled at her expression, and said: 'Come. Consuelo will show you to your room. You will have time to relax before meeting the Duque and his niece.'

Juliet looked down at her dark blue slack suit, and felt relieved. At least she was to have the opportunity of changing before meeting so autocratic a personage as the Duque de Castro.

They entered through heavy doors which stood wide to the morning air, into a hall, marble tiled and panelled with rosewood. A white-painted wrought iron rail supported a wide, shallow staircase, which curved gently up to a long gallery. There were flowers everywhere, on pedestal stands, or simply in huge urns, artistically arranged. There was the smell of beeswax mingled with the perfumes of the flowers, and Juliet thought she would never remember Venterra without recalling the fragrance.

She was looking about her with interest, as Miguel brought in her suitcases, when a dark-skinned woman, with tightly curled hair, approached from along a passage to the left of the hall. Dressed all in black, apart from a white apron, she looked warm and friendly, and Juliet responded to her smile. Was this Consuelo whom Miguel had spoken of?

As though in answer to her unspoken question, Miguel returned at that moment, and standing down the cases he was carrying said: 'Ah, there you are, Consuelo. As you can see, Senhorita Summers has arrived.'

Consuelo eyed the young man with twinkling eyes. 'You are late, Miguel!'

Miguel raised his shoulders indignantly. 'The plane has just landed – is this not right, *senhorita?*' he appealed to Juliet.

Juliet nodded, fingering the strap of her handbag, and Miguel seemed to realize her position, for he said: 'Senhorita Summers, this is Consuelo Rodrigues, housekeeper to the Duque, and my mother's cousin.'

Juliet smiled, and made a perfunctory greeting, and Consuelo folded her arms. 'Welcome to the Quinta de Castro, *senhorita*. I hope you will be very happy here.'

'Why – thank you.' Juliet moved uncomfortably. This was her first taste of being an employee and she was not aware of what was expected of her.

'The Senhorita's room is ready?' questioned Miguel. 'I think she would like to wash and relax for a while before meeting the Duque.'

Consuelo gave a vigorous nod. 'Everything is ready.

Muito obrigado, Miguel. I can manage now. José is waiting for you in the orchard.'

Miguel smiled once more at Juliet. 'I will probably see you later, *senhorita*,' and then he turned and went out through the wide doors.

Juliet sighed after he had gone. His friendliness had been a kind of balm, and now she felt tense and nervous again. Not that Consuelo was an alarming person. With her round, ample girth and beaming face, she seemed amiable enough, and when she picked up two of Juliet's cases and made for the stairs, indicating that Juliet should follow her, Juliet picked up her hand luggage and did so.

The shallow staircase was lined with portraits, and Juliet stared at them, entranced. There were dark, swarthy men and camellia-skinned women, single portraits and family groups, with children dressed in heavy velvets and satins, totally unsuited to the hot Venterra climate. Juliet wondered how long there had been Duques de Castro on the island. Probably for hundreds of years, since the first Spaniards discovered the West Indies. It was a period of history that had always interested her, and her thoughts occupied her to the exclusion of everything else.

Consuelo surged ahead, but Juliet had barely reached the curve of the stairs when footsteps sounded across the tiled courtyard and entered the hall below. She looked down curiously, when a man appeared, wondering who he might be. Tall, dark-haired and deeply tanned, a midnight blue silk shirt open at the throat to reveal the smooth column of his neck rising from the rippling muscles of his chest, he was easily the most attractive male Juliet had ever seen, and she couldn't help but stare until he turned icy grey eyes in her direction.

'*Por deus!*' he swore angrily. 'Miguel was right! Come down here, *senhorita!*'

There was no please or thank you, no apparent sign of anything remotely resembling politeness, and Juliet froze with indignation. The man tapped a slender riding whip against the highly polished leather of his boot.

'Did you hear what I said, *senhorita*?' he asked coldly. 'I am not used to being kept waiting!'

Consuelo had turned now and was coming back down the stairs. 'This is Senhorita Summers, *senhor*,' she said, by way of an introduction.

Juliet stiffened. This then must be her employer, the Duque de Castro. Oh lord, she thought dismally, isn't he charming!

'I am aware of the young woman's name!' the man snapped. '*Senhorita!* Are you paralysed, or merely petrified!'

Juliet felt something flare up inside her at his arrogant words. Just who did he think he was? Just who did he think he was talking to? For a moment she was tempted to reveal her real identity. After all, Robert Lindsay's was a name to be reckoned with in financial circles. And then the temptation died. She doubted whether anything she might say in that direction would achieve more than her instant dismissal. This man lived many miles away from the mercenary capitals of the world, and obviously considered himself a law unto himself.

But she did not intend that he should see that he had either annoyed or disturbed her. With the control of years of training she slowly descended the staircase, until she made contact with the marble floor of the hall. At this level, he was even more overpowering. Tall herself, he was still much taller, with a width of shoulder and a litheness of movement not out of place in an athlete.

'I am neither paralysed nor petrified, *senhor*,' she said, with more confidence than she was feeling. 'I gather you are my employer.'

The man looked down at her with narrowed eyes. 'I am the Duque Felipe Ricardo de Castro, *senhorita*. I do not recall employing *you*!'

For a moment Juliet was nonplussed. Then, gathering her scattered wits, she said: 'I do not understand, *senhor*. I was employed by a firm of solicitors in London, as companion to your niece, a Senhorita Teresa de Castro.'

The man studied her insolently for a moment, then turned to Consuelo. 'You knew about this, Consuelo?'

'*Sim, senhor!*'

'Since when?' he thundered angrily.

'Since two hours ago, Felipe,' remarked a cool voice from the direction of the door which led to the outer patio.

Juliet glanced round and saw a small, slim, attractive woman standing there, dark, like the Duque, with smooth dark hair that clung to the curve of her head like a cap. She was dressed in a delicate shade of cyclamen, and looked cool and sophisticated. She smiled warmly at Juliet, and wrinkled her nose at the Duque.

'Darling, don't be cross,' she continued. 'You know Teresa needs somebody.'

The Duque snapped his fingers furiously. 'I know that you wait until I go riding before telling *my* staff to expect a visitor about whom I know absolutely nothing!' He moved restlessly. 'It is not six months since you employed that American girl, Laura Weston, and after that fiasco I refused to consider anyone else. You knew this, Estelle!'

'*Querido,*' you are embarrassing Senhorita Summers. At least let us have this conversation in private. Consuelo, take Senhorita Summers to her room, and I will speak to the Duque.'

'*Sim, senhora!*' Consuelo turned, but Juliet felt frozen to the spot. This was something neither she nor Rosemary had envisaged. Was her carefully planned ruse to fail because the advertisement had been placed without the Duque's knowledge or condolence? She felt almost numb with incredulity.

Now the Duque turned his dark eyes on her again. He studied her for a moment longer, and then without a word turned and strode across the hall and entered a room at the far side, slamming the door after him.

The woman he had called Estelle continued to look unperturbed. 'Go with Consuelo, *senhorita*. Do not concern yourself with these matters. I can assure you,

27

your job is not in jeopardy.'

Juliet moved at last, and followed Consuelo stiffly up the staircase. She wished she felt as certain. All she could remember was the blatant fury in the man's grey eyes, and the force of his attraction which had hit her like magnetism.

CHAPTER TWO

HER room overlooked the sea, with a balcony on which was a long, low lounger where it would be heaven to sit on hot days. The room, decorated in shades of blue and green and grey, with a bathroom to match, was luxurious and comfortable.

Consuelo stood down her cases, and looked at her with her smiling eyes. 'This is all right, *senhorita?*'

'Oh, yes, thank you, Consuelo. It's wonderful. But—' She halted, and Consuelo looked at her sympathetically.

'The *senhora* means what she says,' she said understandingly. 'The Duque will not dismiss you without reason.'

Juliet sighed and sank down on to the bed. 'But – well, the Duque apparently didn't even know I was coming!'

'No, *senhorita.*'

Juliet frowned. 'That woman – who is she? Is that his wife?'

Consuelo laughed, folding her arms across her heavy breasts. 'No, *senhorita.* The Duque is not married. The Senhora Vinceiro is the widow of his cousin, Pépé. She lives here on Venterra, not far from the *quinta.*'

'I see.' Juliet shook her head, still feeling rather bewildered. 'When – when will I see the Senhorita Teresa?'

'Whenever you are ready, *senhorita*. Senhorita Teresa is with Senhorita Madison at the moment. She has been acting as both nurse and companion since Senhorita Weston was dismissed.'

Juliet had so many questions she wanted to ask. She wanted to know about this fiasco the Duque had spoken about, she wanted to know why Laura Weston had been dismissed, she wanted to know exactly what influence this Estelle Vinceiro had in the *quinta*. She felt almost amused as she recalled her thoughts on the journey here. They had been wholly to do with the problems she had left behind. She had not known she was coming to face far more.

Consuelo moved to the door. 'It is now a little after twelve, *senhorita*. I suggest I bring your lunch to your room, to enable you to unpack and relax for a while. After siesta, which the Senhorita Teresa always takes in her room, I will come and take you to have afternoon tea with her, *sim*?'

Juliet rose to her feet again. 'That sounds delightful, Consuelo, thank you.' She twisted her fingers nervously. 'Do you – do you think the Duque will want to see me again?'

Consuelo spread wide her hands in a typical continental gesture. 'Who can say, *senhorita*? But if you are resting he will not ask me to disturb you. So – I go. If you need anything, ring the bell.'

After Consuelo had gone, Juliet lifted her cases and threw them on the bed. Then she removed the jacket of her suit, and walked lazily on to the balcony. Although she had not been travelling very long this morning, she

30

suddenly felt drained of energy, and she sat down on the lounger and lit a cigarette before attempting to do anything.

In a while, the events of the last few minutes assumed rather less serious proportions, as she saw the amusing side of it all. What a situation! She wished Rosemary were here to share it with her.

A tap at the door heralded the arrival of a young maidservant with a tray containing her lunch. There was a fresh fruit cocktail, pork fried with rice, and a kind of ice cream gateau, followed by coffee and more fruit. It was a very delicious meal, and after she had finished, Juliet felt a little more like work. She opened her cases, hung away her clothes in a capacious fitted wardrobe, and then went into the bathroom to shower before resting on her bed for a while. She had closed her window shutters, and the light slatted through the blinds cast dancing shadows on the ceiling. She watched them for a while, and then her eyelids drooped and she slept.

She awoke refreshed, but startled, with a firm tapping going on at her door. Sliding off the bed, she wrapped herself in a nylon wrapper and opened the door about six inches. Consuelo was outside.

'It is after four, *senhorita*. I have told the Senhorita Teresa you are to have tea with her.'

'Lord!' Juliet gasped. 'I'm sorry, Consuelo, I'm not ready. Will you wait five minutes?'

'Very well, *senhorita*,' Consuelo agreed, but she sounded less than pleased.

Juliet fumbled her way into a white crimplene dress, sleeveless, with a high cuffed neckline, and not too

31

short a skirt. Her hair, immaculately pleated earlier, now hung in wisps and with careless fingers she wrenched out the hairgrips and brushed it savagely. It fell, thick and straight to her shoulders, sherry-coloured and very attractive. Cursing to herself for sleeping so long, she began to wind it back into its pleat, when Consuelo tapped again.

'*Senhorita*,' she said persistently, 'please hurry.'

Juliet lost control of the hair, and it fell loose again. 'Oh, blast, blast, blast!' she exclaimed angrily, and then with decision, she combed it smooth and looked at her reflection disconsolately. It was no good. She needed plenty of time and patience to dress it in the pleat, and anyway, she might be going to get the sack, so what did it matter?

She emerged from the bedroom and Consuelo looked at her in surprise. 'Such pretty hair, *senhorita*,' she exclaimed delightedly.

Juliet looked rueful. 'But rather impractical,' she said, smiling. 'I'm sorry I kept you waiting, Consuelo. I fell asleep, I'm afraid.'

Consuelo seemed unperturbed now. 'It is the climate,' she said, firmly. 'Most have the siesta! It is a good idea, *sim*?'

'Hmm,' agreed Juliet enthusiastically, feeling more ready to face any challenge which might come her way.

They descended the main staircase to the wide hall, and then out on to the patio that surrounded the central courtyard. The patio was tiled with mosaic in a variety of colours, while tubs of flamboyants and the ever-present climbing bougainvillea added their own tropical beauty to the scene. A glass-topped table supported a jug, some ice cubes and several glasses, and beside this table a girl was sitting in a wheelchair, glancing carelessly through a magazine. As though aware of another presence, she turned and looked at Juliet, and Consuelo murmured something about getting the tea and left them.

The girl was dark, like her uncle, with long hair worn in a single braid over one shoulder. But her expression was remote and perhaps a little sulky, and Juliet advanced towards her with some trepidation.

'Hello,' she said, in a friendly fashion. 'You must be Teresa. My name is – Rosemary.' She almost slipped up altogether and said Juliet.

The girl viewed her critically, putting aside her magazine. 'Who else would I be?' she asked pointedly, glancing down at the wheelchair.

Juliet drew a little closer. 'Yes, perhaps it was a stupid remark. However, I couldn't think of any other way of introducing myself.'

Teresa's eyes flickered for a moment, and then she resumed her sullen expression. 'Where have you come from? London?'

'Yes, that's right.'

'Estelle never gives up, does she?' Teresa gave a short laugh.

Juliet deemed it better not to answer this. She had no desire to take sides without first knowing all the circumstances of the case. So she seated herself in a basketwork chair, also placed near the table, and sighed. 'What a beautiful place this is. You must love it here.'

Teresa shrugged her thin shoulders, and Juliet noticed how painfully thin she really was. 'It's all right,' she said. She spoke with little accent, and Juliet could only assume she had attended a British school. 'It's better than hospital, anyway.'

Juliet bit her lip. 'Yes. Were you in hospital long?'

'Long enough.' Teresa was scrutinizing her intently. 'What did you used to do, before you came here?'

Juliet felt the colour seeping into her cheeks. 'Well, I – er – this and that!'

Teresa sniffed. 'Why did you come here? Did you think it would make a nice holiday.'

'No.' Juliet was swift to deny this. 'No. I came because there was an advertisement in a British newspaper and I thought the job sounded interesting.' This at least was true.

Teresa wrinkled her nose. 'I hear my uncle did not exactly welcome you with open arms.'

Juliet had to smile at this. 'That's true,' she answered.

'I expect he was good and mad,' said Teresa, a little enthusiasm entering her voice now. 'After the last time!'

Juliet did not ask the question that trembled on her tongue, but Teresa went on: 'Estelle keeps trying to get me off her neck, you know! I think she's jealous!' This was said with some satisfaction.

Juliet frowned. 'Jealous? Senhora Vinceiro? Why should she be jealous?' This was one question she could not help but ask. She was only human after all.

Teresa fingered the pleat of the blue skirt she was wearing. 'Estelle wants Felipe – it's as simple as that! She wanted him ten years ago when she married his cousin because he lived on Venterra also, and my uncle was obviously not prepared to marry her then. And Pépé – her husband – died two years ago, he was years older than Estelle, of course, and she was granted her wish. To live on Venterra – and to have a second chance with my uncle.'

Juliet swallowed hard. This – from a sixteen-year-old!

'I think you're dramatizing the situation, Teresa,' she said, glancing round with relief as the young maid appeared with the tray of tea.

'I am not!' Teresa sounded angry. 'Estelle hated it when Felipe brought me here, installing me in his house, making her plans doubly difficult.'

'Oh really,' exclaimed Juliet disbelievingly. 'You're his niece!'

'Only by marriage,' retorted Teresa, at once. 'My father was not Felipe's brother. My mother had been married before. My father died ten years ago. He suffered from heart disease.'

'I see.' Juliet thanked the maid, and stood up. 'Shall – shall I handle this?'

Teresa nodded with some dignity. 'Of course now I am an orphan. And family ties are strong among Portuguese families. I am just as much Felipe's responsibility whether my relationship to him is distant or otherwise.'

'I see,' said Juliet again. Heavens, she thought to herself, what a situation!

The tea was weak, but hot, and the wafer-thin biscuits rather delicious. Teresa drank one cup of tea, but ate nothing, and Juliet felt greedy because she ate three biscuits. Conversation lapsed, and Juliet wondered what was going through the girl's head. She was obviously obsessed with intrigue, seeing herself as a kind of innocent charmer, who couldn't help but annoy a woman like Estelle Vinceiro. She seemed to imagine – *what*? That the Duque was perhaps attracted to her – or merely just sympathetic towards her. Did she imagine Estelle Vinceiro's jealousy, if indeed it was jealousy, was based on truth? It was incredible! Juliet knew little, and had seen less, of the Duque as yet, but she could swear he was a man in his late thirties, and not some impressionable boy. Oh, it was ridiculous!

Teresa replaced her cup in its saucer, and placing it on the table said: 'Is my uncle going to allow you to stay?'

Juliet hesitated. 'I – er – I'm not quite sure. Why shouldn't he allow me to stay, after all? You do require companionship, don't you?'

'No.' Teresa was vehement. 'Felipe is all the companionship I need.'

'But at some time, someone did think you needed companionship,' exclaimed Juliet patiently. 'Or the advertisement would never have been devised.'

'Estelle did it – it's all her doing!' said Teresa hotly. 'She wants to provide me with a companion, so that Felipe will have more time for her. *Odio* Estelle!'

'Teresa!' Juliet started at the sound of that voice. '*Que faz voce?*'

'Oh, Tio Felipe,' Teresa held out her hands to him, and lapsed into her own language, speaking appealingly, her dark eyes wide and innocent, so that Juliet began to wonder just what she was telling him.

The Duque had changed now into a cream silk lounge suit, that enhanced the swarthy cast of his complexion. The close-fitting trousers suited the muscular length of his legs, while Juliet was surprised to see that the jacket was quite modern in design with a long centre back vent. She supposed she had expected Venterra to be quite out of touch with civilization, but a man like Duque Felipe Ricardo de Castro was hardly likely to allow anyone but a Savile Row tailor to dress him. Trying to view him emotionlessly was difficult; his personality was such that she was intensely aware of him as a force to be reckoned with.

Teresa had paused now, and he straightened from the lounging position he had adopted near Teresa's chair, and looked straight at Juliet.

'So, *senhorita*,' he murmured, taking out a case of cheroots and placing one between his firm lips, 'you have perhaps discovered that not everything you read in the newspapers is true.' His tone was cool, but mocking.

Juliet frowned, resisting the impulse to jump to her feet. 'Do you mean the advertisement, *senhor?*' she questioned, at last.

The Duque inclined his head, lighting his cheroot from a slim gold lighter. 'Of course. You have been –

how shall I put it? – misled! I regret the circumstance, of course, but . . .' He shrugged his broad shoulders.

Juliet digested this, and then deemed she would feel at less of a disadvantage if she did stand up. Getting to her feet, she said, rather unsteadily: 'You – you regret the circumstance, *senhor*! Are you trying to tell me my services are not required?'

'How perceptive of you, Senhorita Summers,' he murmured lazily. 'That is exactly what I mean.'

Juliet took a deep breath. So much for Estelle Vinceiro's influence, she thought gloomily.

'Might – might I ask why?' she said, rather tremulously.

The Duque frowned now. He was obviously not used to having anyone question his commands. He glanced down at Teresa thoughtfully, and then said:

'I think, *senhorita*, we might discuss this in my study. I realize you feel annoyed and inconvenienced, but I trust I can compensate you financially for any inconvenience caused. Come!' His tone was peremptory now, and Juliet obeyed, even while she felt furious that he should imagine he could buy her off.

He led the way through the marble-floored hall, along a corridor whose windows faced a rose garden, into a room furnished austerely in dark wood and leather, and whose walls were lined with leather-tooled books. He walked round to the far side of the desk which commanded a central position after he had closed the door and indicated that Juliet should sit in the chair opposite. She did so with some trepidation, which increased when he himself did not sit down but stood regarding her with dark, sombre eyes. If he found anything attractive in Juliet's smooth, lightly tanned features, in the widely spaced depths of her eyes, or in the sun-kissed lustre of her hair, he did not show it, and merely seemed to be absorbed with some inner thoughts.

'Now,' he said, at last, when the tension Juliet was feeling had become almost a tangible thing, 'it is too late today for you to consider making the journey back to Barbados, and from there home to England. However, tomorrow I will have the hydroplane ready and waiting for you at ten o'clock.'

Something inside Juliet snapped at his words. She had been accustomed all her life to fighting for anything she wanted, and she saw no reason to stop now. This chance would never come her way again. Once her father discovered what she had done he would never trust her completely again. She would never be sure, wherever she went, that he had not got someone tailing her, monitoring her every movement. It was already too late to get back without his finding out what she had done. Rosemary had a letter to post two days after her departure which explained a little of her actions, without actually giving her whereabouts away. It would put both Mandy and her father's minds at rest, and prevent Robert Lindsay from calling the police.

But this man, this arrogant Duque, was attempting, with casual apologies, to ruin everything she had struggled to achieve, as well as turning a blind eye to the situation that was developing under his very nose.

Couldn't he see what was happening to Teresa? Didn't he feel the emotion she was harbouring for him? Or did he indeed know what was going on, and found it satisfying to his ego?

Juliet wasn't sure, all she was sure of was that in this, at least, Estelle Vinceiro was right. She linked her fingers, bent her head, and exploded her bombshell.

'Are you aware that your niece is in love with you?'

The Duque had been waiting for her reply, flicking through the correspondence on his desk idly, but at her words, his head jerked up, and he stared at her with incensed dark eyes. Juliet shivered, and returned her own gaze to her fingers, wondering however she had dared suggest such a thing.

'*Senhorita*, your remarks may be a product of your indignation at your dismissal, but they are in extremely bad taste!'

Juliet bit her lip hard. What the hell, he was firing her anyway, what had she got to lose?

'Bad taste or not, they're true,' she retorted, allowing her eyes to meet his momentarily. 'Why do you suppose she objects to a companion? Because it limits the time you might spend with her!'

'Enough! *Deus!* No one has ever spoken to me like this! How do you know these things? You have been here less than twelve hours! Have you, in that time, assimilated our positions so perfectly?'

The Duque walked round the desk restlessly, making Juliet acutely aware of him as a man, with a man's powers, and she was treading on dangerous ground, even if she was leaving in the morning. Here, the Duque Felipe Ricardo de Castro was all powerful. Who would help her, if he chose to punish her for her outspokenness? She shivered, and wished she had a cigarette.

He returned to his position behind the desk at last, relieving a little of her tension, and again studied her intently.

'*Senhorita*, I have considered what you have said, and I find I simply cannot believe you. *Por Deus*, Teresa is but sixteen years of age; I am nearing my fortieth birthday. Such a liaison can never have occurred to a child like that. I have never, at any time, given her any reason—' He halted, and stiffened. 'Wait! I will not explain myself to you. You will leave tomorrow, as I have said.'

Juliet sighed, and rose to her feet. 'Very well, *senhor*,' she said, not without some annoyance. 'Maybe the next – companion – you employ will not be treated so carelessly.'

'There will be no more companions,' replied the Duque coldly.

'There may have to be,' retorted Juliet, her cheeks flushed. 'In another year, regardless of her disablement, Teresa will be ready for marriage, and you may find your position less tenable!' She marched to the door, but despite his greater weight he was there before her, leaning against the door, preventing her escape.

'Wait!' he muttered sombrely. 'Wait! Maybe I have been too hasty. Maybe you are right. Maybe Teresa does need a companion after all. You are not the first person to tell me so. Does not my own cousin-in-law advocate your arguments also?' He straightened, looking down at her with enigmatic eyes. 'Very well, *senhorita*, you may stay. At least for a month. We will discover at the end of that time whether your presence has created any special improvement. *Sim?*'

Juliet's legs felt weak. She didn't know whether it was the relief at knowing she was staying, or the Duque's proximity, but she suddenly seemed breathless and completely enervated.

'Ver – very well, *senhor*,' she murmured, and then, as though common sense asserted itself, she said: 'What – what are you going to tell Teresa?' She moved slightly away from him, pressing her hands together, as a demon of disobedience urged her to continue: 'This is always supposing I agree.'

The Duque caught his breath in an angry gasp. 'Are you even daring to suggest you might not stay?' he ground out.

Juliet shrugged, maintaining her calm attitude with the utmost difficulty. 'Well, after all, you seem to imagine you can dismiss me and then re-employ me without even considering my feelings. Oh, I agree, I did suggest that Teresa did require a companion, and I was angry that you should think you could return me to London like some unwanted parcel, *senhor*, but even I have feelings, and as a woman I deserve a little more consideration!'

'*O que hei-de eu fazer?* You are the most exasperating creature I have ever met!' he muttered angrily.

'As for you being a woman, you are little more than a child yourself!'

'I am twenty-one, *senhor*, and no more a child than your — your cousin's widow, Senhora Vinceiro!' Juliet disliked his assumption intensely.

The Duque pressed out his cheroot violently in a copper ashtray, and then stared at her coldly. 'So, *senhorita*! May I have your decision? Or do you require time to think about it? I warn you, I may yet change my own opinion!'

Juliet felt her cheeks burning. 'I'll stay—' then, as he would have spoken, she went on, 'providing you tell me a little more about Teresa, and her condition, and the reasons for your antipathy towards a companion for her!'

She was amazed at her own temerity, and so apparently was the Duque. He lit another cheroot, and then crossed to a tray of drinks on a nearby table. He poured himself a large whisky, but drank it at one gulp before turning to Juliet and asking her whether she would care for a drink herself. Juliet shook her head, and he raised his eyebrows mockingly.

'Surely English women are completely emancipated, are they not?'

'I've just drank two cups of tea, *senhor*,' replied Juliet coolly, marvelling at her own composure.

'*Touché!*' He half-smiled, revealing even white teeth, and Juliet felt a strange sensation disturb the pit of her stomach. It was not an unpleasant sensation, and yet it frightened her a little, and she was glad when he seated himself behind the desk, and resumed his lazy scrutiny of the papers on his desk.

Juliet hovered uncertainly by the door, and he nodded to the chair opposite him. 'Do sit down, *senhorita*, or I shall have to stand myself, and this may take a few minutes.'

Juliet subsided into the chair again, and linked her hands in her lap, the demure attitude belying the strength of her convictions.

'So, *senhorita*,' he began, 'I will tell you about Teresa. As you know she is sixteen years of age, and reasonably intelligent. Prior to the accident she attended an academy in Lisbon, my brother lived near there, you understand, but on her parents' death, and her own subsequent disability, she was brought here — by me.' He drew on his cheroot. 'Teresa was not my brother's child, but the child of his wife, and her first husband.'

'Yes, Teresa told me,' replied Juliet, and he frowned.

'I see. She must have been singularly confiding this afternoon. Still — as I have said, after the accident, I brought her here. There was no one else. Her mother's family — parents, at least, were dead, she had no brothers or sisters. The child was quite alone. Naturally, as she had taken my brother's name, she was as much his child as any blood relation could be.'

'I see.'

'The accident — it was tragic. The usual motorway pile-up, with Teresa trapped in the wreckage for hours. Hours when she was conscious, and suffered much mental torture.' He sighed. 'The hospital could find little wrong with her; there is no injury to her legs, no spinal damage, she simply refuses to walk! It is as simple – or maybe, as difficult – as that!' He leant forward. 'And that is why I do not wish her to become emotionally disturbed, in any direction! She already is disturbed, and only time, and affection, and patience can cure her. She has a nurse, Miss Madison is a very capable woman. But she is old, in her fifties, and consequently can provide little companionship to a girl of Teresa's age.'

Juliet sighed. 'Then why create so much difficulty about employing a companion for her?' she exclaimed.

The Duque frowned. 'You are a very curious young woman, Miss Summers. I do not know that I care for your attitude!'

Juliet's colour deepened. 'Why? Don't you like plain speaking?'

'Plain speaking? What is this? The right to be impertinent if one so desires?'

'No. It's just being truthful, and calling black black.'

'Hmm! Well, I will reserve judgment, *senhorita*.'

'And are you going to tell me why you refused to employ me?' Juliet determined to have it all out with him.

He shrugged. 'Estelle did it all, *senhorita*. As she did before. Only then the girl was an American, Laura Weston. It was a disaster. Teresa disliked her, and there were continual bouts of disharmony in the household. In addition – oh, well, that at least is of no interest to you. So, *senhorita*, what do you think now?'

Juliet sighed. 'Of course I should like the job,' she admitted. 'Teresa presents a challenge. I never could resist a challenge.'

He smiled, this time without mockery. 'You have courage, *pequena*.'

Juliet wished he had said nothing. There was that awful sensation in her stomach again. She got hastily to her feet.

'Do you want me to tell Teresa?' she asked.

'A moment,' he answered, rising also. 'Tell me, your remark at the commencement of our discussion – what exactly did you mean?'

'What remark?' Juliet pretended not to understand him.

The Duque's frown returned. 'You know exactly which remark,' he averred coldly. 'You said that Teresa imagined herself in love with me.'

'I said she *was* in love with you,' replied Juliet quietly, bending her head. 'At sixteen, a girl like Teresa is very intense.'

'And you really believe there is some truth in this?'

'Of course.' Juliet looked at him. 'It's simple really. Child psychology, if you like. You represent everything to her. You rescued her from a life of loneliness and possible poverty, and brought her to an island rich in beauty and wealth. How else could she regard you but as a kind of knight in shining armour! In addition, you apparently spend much time with her, entertaining her, charming her!' Juliet shrugged. 'She is an im-

46

pressionable creature, *senhor*. And without friends, which is very important.'

He chewed his cheroot savagely. 'And what would you have me do, *senhorita*? Ignore her?'

'No. That would be unnecessarily cruel. If I stay, I should like your permission to cultivate friends for Teresa among children of her own age group. Maybe then she will realize how – well, futile, are her hopes.'

The Duque nodded thoughtfully. 'Yes, I suppose you are right again.' He gave a short exclamation in his own language. 'It seems I may yet have reason to be grateful to you, *senhorita*.'

Juliet walked to the door, and then looked back. 'And Teresa? Shall I tell her?'

The Duque hesitated, and then shook his head. 'No, I suppose not. This is something I must do. I suggest you wait until the morning before you present yourself again to my niece. She may not appreciate your company today.'

Juliet thought this was a vast understatement. Teresa would very likely hate her as she already hated Estelle Vinceiro. Juliet felt a faint feeling of sympathy towards the Duque's cousin-in-law. Obviously, she was as aware of Teresa's affections as Juliet was.

The Duque watched her open the door, and then said: 'I am dining out this evening, but I will probably see you tomorrow to ascertain your progress. *Boa tarde, senhorita*.'

Juliet said good afternoon, went along the corridor to the main hall, and up the stairs to her room. Once there, she collapsed weakly on the bed, unable for a moment to grasp everything that had happened during the last half hour or so. It was incredible that she had had the courage to speak so fearlessly to the Duque, and yet it had worked, and she had won her small victory.

She slid off the bed and walked to the window, and out on to the balcony. Here the ground shelved away below her to low dunes and then to the beach. The smooth, silky waters of the Caribbean lapped on sand that was warm and inviting. She leaned on the balcony rail, revelling in the warmth of the sun, inhaling the fragrance of the climbing plants that grew in such abundance. A palm was within reach of her fingers, with broad leaves looking as though they had been newly polished. Was it only this morning that she had arrived? It seemed much longer than that. And despite the uncertainty of all that had happened, she knew she wanted to stay.

CHAPTER THREE

She slept soundly and awoke next morning to the shrill sounds of the sea birds crying, and the gentle roar of the waves on the grey rocks. Sliding out of bed, she went first to the window, throwing wide the shutters, and stepping out on to the balcony. Although it was early, the air was warm, and taking a deep breath she smoothed her hair behind her ears, allowing the atmosphere to envelop her in its warmth and fragrance. She could hear the sounds of activity emanating from the servants' quarters, and the melodious singing voice of one of the gardeners working in the formal gardens which flanked the front entrance. Her room was on that side of the building that faced the sea, but away to the left among the density of trees that backed the *quinta*, she could see outbuildings which might be garages or stables. Obviously the Duque rode; yesterday, at the time of her first encounter with him, he had been wearing riding clothes, and she remembered the whip very well that he had held in his slim brown hand.

Thrusting thoughts of the Duque away, she tried to estimate the distance out to the bows of a sleek, white yacht, that lay at anchor in the bay. This part of the island seemed sparsely populated, although probably there were villages which did not encroach too closely on the private environs of the *quinta*. She wondered whether there were many other European families on the island, and if so, how they amused themselves. Of course, with the Duque's resources, he could visit Barbados or St. Vincent or Martinique, for entertainment. She sighed. Of course, with all the outdoor facilities available, like riding, skin-diving, water-skiing and sailing, together with the more prosaic pastimes like tennis, golf or fishing, there was plenty to occupy the time. Hadn't her father always maintained that the West Indies provided the best of both worlds, a temperate, yet a sunny and dry climate?

Turning back into the room, she entered the bathroom, and was just drying herself after a shower, when there was a knock at the outer door. Calling 'Come in,' she peeped round the bathroom door in time to see a young maid leaving a tray on her bedside table.

'Oh, thank you,' said Juliet, smiling, tucking a towel securely round her, and coming into the bedroom. 'Where does Miss – I mean, Senhorita Teresa usually have her breakfast?'

The maid frowned. 'Senhorita Teresa eat on – er – patio,' she said, with difficulty, and then smiled at her achievement. '*Sim?*'

'Thank you,' Juliet nodded, and poured herself a glass of fresh fruit juice from the jug on the tray. It was a mixture of orange and lemon and lime, and was delicious. The maid left her, and Juliet dressed in a short red pleated skirt, and a white blouse, with three-quarter-length sleeves, and a demure cuffed neck. She spent several minutes securing her hair, deciding it was easier to braid it first, before attempting to put it up. Then, after two cups of coffee from the coffee jug which was also on the tray, she collected the tray and left her room.

Although the *quinta* was large, she had no difficulty in finding her way to the main hall, for a glance out of the windows confirmed her whereabouts. When she had brought Juliet's dinner to her room the previous evening, Consuelo had given her a brief outline of the layout of the building, and now Juliet knew that Teresa had her rooms in that side of the building furthest from the sea because she did not like the sound of the waves. Juliet was obviously not to be encouraged to leave her room, she had thought a little dryly, when Consuelo arrived with the tray, but the housekeeper had explained that as the Duque was out, and Teresa was dining in her room with Senhorita Madison, her nurse, it would have been a lonely meal downstairs in the dining room. Even so, Juliet had taken the opportunity after dinner, of taking a walk in the gardens, enjoying the scents and sounds of the night, her senses stirred by the sound of a calypso band playing not too far distant. She thought that perhaps a party was going on in one of the villas further round the coast, and she had felt a faint pang of envy.

But this morning, all that was forgotten, and she was even beginning to wonder, with something less than fear, what her father had done about her letter. No doubt he would be furious, and she hoped when he saw Rosemary he would not treat her to one of his furious rampages. Not that Rosemary wasn't more than capable of dealing with him; she was a very sensible and determined young woman.

Juliet now found her way to the kitchens, and left the tray with the smiling maid, who confirmed that Senhorita Teresa was already on the patio. When Juliet emerged from the building, she found Teresa had started her breakfast, a simple meal of fruit and rolls accompanied by fruit juice, and did not even look up when Juliet came to join her at the table.

'Good morning, Teresa,' said Juliet lightly. 'Did you sleep well?'

Teresa did not answer, and Juliet poured herself a cup of coffee, and told the maid who had appeared that she too would have fruit and rolls. When the maid had gone, she sipped her coffee thoughtfully, viewing the young girl over the rim of her cup, wondering what thoughts were at present torturing Teresa's mind. Teresa was studiously avoiding looking at her, concentrating on her meal with intense single-mindedness.

Juliet accepted the rolls the maid brought her, buttered one and began to pare a peach slowly. She looked across at Teresa's bent head, and said: 'Are you going to maintain this silence indefinitely? Or will you tell me what is annoying you and be done with it?'

Teresa gave her a scornful glance, but still refused to speak. Juliet's appetite deteriorated. This was hopeless! If the Duque appeared now and saw Teresa's reaction he would imagine the worst.

'For heaven's sake, I thought you pretended to be adult!' she exclaimed, realizing that only by antagonizing Teresa would she produce any reaction at all.

Teresa's glass clattered as it hit the glass surface of the table. 'Don't try to infuriate me!' she snapped coldly. 'Your presence here can produce nothing but dislike between us! I told you I didn't want you here – and that still stands!'

Juliet swallowed a mouthful of coffee. 'I see. Is there something about me that you particularly dislike, or is it just companions in general?'

Teresa gave her a doubtful look. 'Stop trying to be clever! I don't know what you said to Felipe, but whatever it was you won't persuade me as you appear to have persuaded him!'

'Your uncle realizes that you need company – of your own age!'

'You're not my age!'

'I know. But I'm a lot nearer your age than anyone else here!'

'So what? You know nothing about me! I don't particularly get along with – with – women!'

'Don't you? Oh, that is a disappointment!' Juliet's voice was slightly teasing. 'Then we'll have to see about getting you some – boy-friends.'

'Don't you dare!' Teresa's face was flushed now. 'If you're thinking of bringing some of the other boys and girls on the island here to meet me, forget it! I won't see them!'

'Why not?' Juliet was curious in spite of herself.

'Because they bore me stiff!'

Juliet frowned. 'How do you know? If you've never met them?'

'I don't want to meet anybody.'

'Oh, I see.' Juliet looked thoughtful.

Teresa seemed to get more annoyed at this. 'Now don't go imagining it's because I'm in a wheelchair!' she exclaimed. 'My condition hasn't altered anything. I never did like – *boys!*'

Juliet compressed her lips. Teresa seemed completely self-sufficient. Why was it that she sensed that she was not?

Changing the subject, she said: 'Well, as we are here, and I am staying, what shall we do this morning?'

Teresa finished her fruit juice, and wiped her mouth on her napkin. 'I don't know what you're doing – I'm going to sit here and read, and listen to my radio.'

Juliet sighed. 'Oh, is that so? What if I insist that you accompany me?'

Teresa frowned. 'You couldn't!'

'Oh, couldn't I?' Juliet ran her tongue over her lips. 'I think I could. Your uncle has made me your companion – and I mean to be just that!'

Teresa gripped the arms of her chair. 'You can't force me to do anything,' she exclaimed hotly.

'No, not force exactly!' Juliet finished the peach, drained her coffee cup, and then lit a cigarette, savouring it lazily. 'Tell me, Teresa, do you swim?'

'No!'

'Why not?' Juliet blew a smoke-ring into the air. 'Can't you?'

'I could – I did, until I had my accident.' Teresa

bent her head.

'You ought not to be reminding her of that, Miss Summers,' remarked a woman's voice in an accent that could only be American.

Juliet glanced round interestedly. So this was Miss Madison, Teresa's nurse. As the Duque had said, she was a much older woman, slim and gaunt-looking, her greying hair drawn back into a tight knot. Not a very inspiring companion for a rebellious sixteen-year-old.

'You must be Miss Madison,' said Juliet now. 'I'm pleased to meet you. However, I don't think there's any point in hedging about something which must have become quite inescapable to a girl as imaginative as Teresa.'

The older woman came to stand before her. 'Are you qualified to give psychiatric opinions, Miss Summers?' she asked coldly.

Lord, thought Juliet, another one!

Aloud, she said: 'No. Not at all. Merely imaginative myself!'

'What do you mean?'

'Simply that keeping Teresa a prisoner of her own thoughts never helped anyone!' Juliet controlled the ready flow of words she felt like uttering. Instead, she said: 'I've just been suggesting that Teresa ought to swim. It might give her confidence in the use of her limbs.'

Miss Madison stiffened. 'Teresa has never wanted to do any of these things, and it is not good for her to be upset.'

55

Teresa was watching this interchange with some enjoyment, and Juliet knew it.

'I don't think Teresa gets upset as easily as all that,' she replied, praying she was right. 'Anyway, as I shall be here to keep her company, we may yet persuade her – betweeen us.'

'I am employed as Teresa's nurse,' replied Miss Madison coldly. 'The Duque gives me my orders. When he suggests that Teresa ought to go swimming then I will endeavour to accomplish it.'

Fiddlesticks, thought Juliet impatiently, but she merely smiled, and refrained from replying.

The nurse seated herself beside Teresa, and began to speak to her in fluent Portuguese. Juliet wrinkled her nose, and said:

'Do you mind? I don't speak Portuguese. What are you telling Teresa now?'

Miss Madison gave her a haughty glance. 'I suggest you attempt to learn the language, Miss Summers, if you intend to stay here. The Duque probably thinks you speak fluent Portuguese, as I do. Of course, as Senhora Vinceiro hired you I don't suppose she bothered to find out. So long as Teresa is out of her way, she will be happy.'

Juliet felt a sneaking sympathy for Estelle Vinceiro. She also felt disturbed at what Nurse Madison said. Her words had proved where her sympathies lay, and Juliet doubted whether it was good for Teresa to have a woman so obviously willing to console her as her constant companion. Still, this was only her second day on the island, and it was far too soon to begin wreaking havoc with the Duque's employees.

Getting to her feet, she left them, walking across the courtyard to the fountain and trailing her fingers in the cool water. It was a beautiful morning, much too nice to spend cooped up in the *quinta*.

With decision, she turned and said to Teresa: 'Does your uncle have a car which you can use if ever you want to go down to the village?'

Teresa frowned. 'There is an estate car which is seldom used. Why?'

'You and I are going out. You can take me on a guided tour of the island.'

Nurse Madison got to her feet. 'Teresa usually spends some time with me during the mornings, *senhorita*. There are exercises—'

'I think we can leave them just for one morning, don't you?' remarked Juliet sweetly. 'And please, call me Rosemary – or *Miss* Summers. Although I am sure your Portuguese is impeccable, calling me *senhorita* is really carrying things too far, don't you think?'

Then she was sorry for her impetuosity. After all, Nurse Madison was not a young woman, and it was difficult adapting to change so quickly at her age. However, Nurse Madison merely turned and marched towards the entrance of the building, giving one parting shot as she went.

'The Duque is out this morning, *Miss* Summers, but I shall certainly see him on his return about your responsibilities here. I do not care to be given orders by a chit of a girl!'

'Oh, heavens!' exclaimed Juliet, but Nurse Madison was gone.

'You've done it now, haven't you,' remarked Teresa, with some satisfaction. 'Felipe may be persuaded that I need a companion for my own good, but making an enemy of Nurse Madison is much different.'

Juliet felt like stamping her foot with annoyance, but instead she retained the smile on her face with difficulty, and said, firmly: 'Nevertheless, Senhorita de Castro, we do have this morning at our disposal, and I intend that we should use it as I think fit. It's not good for you, remaining here, living the life of seclusion. As I suggested, you are going to show me the island.'

'Make me!' Teresa scowled angrily, and Juliet sighed and then took charge of the wheelchair.

'It may seem cruel, Teresa,' she said, as Teresa protested volubly in her own language at the liberties Juliet was taking, 'but sometimes we have to be cruel to be kind!'

Miguel was only too willing to supply them with a car. He also lifted the kicking Teresa into it, putting her in front beside Juliet, who had taken charge of the wheel.

'Tell me,' said Juliet, when they were both in the car, and Miguel still leaned against the bonnet, 'which is the best way to go? Just in case my companion chooses to remain a silent one!'

Miguel grinned cheerfully, his eyes appraising the young girl unashamedly, and then returning to Juliet's fair beauty. 'Maybe I should come with you, *senhorita*?' he suggested.

Juliet shook her head. 'I think not,' she said a little dryly. 'I have quite enough problems as it is.'

Miguel advised her to take the coast route which circled the island. 'It is the most attractive,' he said, putting a hand up to shade his eyes. 'If you continue towards Miscaela, a village further along from here, you will see a sign for Venterra Montanah. It is a place in the hills where there is a small inn. They make the most delicious coffee!' He kissed his fingers extravagantly.

'Well, thank you, Miguel,' said Juliet, and smiled at Teresa who refused to meet her eyes but sat staring mutinously at her own fingers.

Yet, in spite of Teresa's silence, and the obvious atmosphere she created, Juliet enjoyed the drive. Miscaela was just a fishing village as Miguel had said, but Venterra Montanah was something special. The inn was situated on the edge of a cliff, almost hanging over the valley below. To get there Juliet had to negotiate some of the worst bends she had ever encountered, and even Teresa held on to her seat, her face flushed with apprehension at times. But it was all worth it, and although Teresa could not get out of the car, Juliet parked it overlooking the valley so that they could see the view while they had coffee, and continental pastries.

Teresa ate the pastries, drank her coffee, but said nothing, in spite of Juliet's several attempts to get her to do so. She hoped she had not done any harm, bringing the girl up here. If she were emotionally disturbed still from the accident, Juliet was surprised. To her, all

Teresa's emotions were generated from a genuine affection towards the man who had brought her to Venterra. And after all, that really was her job: to help destroy that particular illusion of Teresa's, not pander to it.

The journey down was almost as hair-raising, although by then Juliet had foreknowledge of the curves. They arrived back at the *quinta* soon after twelve-thirty, and as Consuelo had told her that lunch was no until one-thirty, Juliet thought she had timed everything perfectly.

Miguel was there to restore Teresa to her wheelchair, which he did very capably, and despite Teresa's attitude, Juliet took charge of it again, wheeling her through the arched entrance into the courtyard, and across to the patio where the Duque was standing, leaning against a balcony pillar, talking to the small dark woman Juliet had seen only briefly the day before, Estelle Vinceiro.

He straightened at their approach, and gave Juliet the benefit of his inscrutable gaze. 'You have been out, *senhorita*?'

Teresa did not allow Juliet to answer before she burst into speech, a stream of incoherent Portuguese that seemed anything but polite. But this time the Duque raised his hand, and said:

'Speak English, Teresa. As Senhorita Summers stays here at my instigation we will not ignore her presence.'

Teresa cast a malevolent glance at Estelle Vinceiro, and then, putting her hands on the manipulating wheels of her chair, she moved across to the Duque.

'Senhorita Summers made me accompany her on a sightseeing tour of the island!' she exclaimed tremulously.

'Is this so, *senhorita*?' The Duque frowned.

Juliet heaved a sigh. 'Yes, of course. Why not? Teresa needs to get away from the *quinta* sometimes. It is not good for her to be cloistered here.'

The Duque's lips thinned. 'Did it occur to you, *senhorita*, that Teresa may not yet find travelling in a car acceptable?'

'Acceptable?' Juliet bit her lip. 'Do you mean because of her accident?'

'Of course.'

'Then I would have thought the sooner she got used to travelling in a car again, the better,' said Juliet quickly. 'If Teresa is still disturbed, which I personally doubt, by car riding, then she should endeavour to overcome the feeling, not pander to it!'

'I agree.' Estelle Vinceiro crossed her slim legs smoothly. 'Felipe, don't imagine your niece is made of sugar, she will not melt away.'

The Duque drew out his case of cheroots and put one between his lips. 'And you, Teresa? What have you to say to that?'

Teresa looked mutinous. 'I did not want to go out, Tio Felipe. I like being here – you know I do. You already know my opinion concerning Senhorita Summers.'

Estelle sighed now. 'Oh, Teresa, must we go into all that again? You are a spoiled *doninha*!'

'Estelle!' The Duque's voice was angry now.

'*Desculpe-me*, Felipe, but your niece is not the easiest person to be friendly with!' She rose to her feet, sliding an arm through his. 'Please, Felipe, forgive me!'

Teresa's face was incensed, Juliet could see. Her jealousy was eating her up, and Juliet couldn't see any immediate improvement occurring here. It would take time to make Teresa realize the futility of her hopes. What she didn't understand was her own feelings when she saw Estelle Vinceiro attempting to charm the Duque. That awful twisted feeling had returned, and deciding action was the only course, she said:

'If you'll excuse me, *senhor, senhora*, I will wash before lunch.'

The Duque released himself from Estelle's clinging fingers, and said: 'One more moment, *senhorita*. Nurse Madison tells me you have been interfering in her arrangements with Teresa.'

Juliet stiffened, halted, and turned to face him. 'Yes, I have.'

'Might I ask why?'

'You can ask, *senhor*, but whether my answer will appeal to you I cannot say!'

'*Senhorita!*' His voice was warning, now.

'Very well. Nurse Madison is a middle-aged woman, quite out of touch I would think with modern nursing methods.'

'It is not the easiest thing to do – to find a nurse, fully qualified, who is willing to leave all the advantages of civilization and come and live on an island miles from anywhere,' retorted the Duque coolly. 'Nurse Madison was qualified, and reliable.'

'What you mean is, you requested an older person,' inserted Estelle, with a piquant smile at the Duque. She turned to Juliet. 'Senhorita Summers, my – er – cousin is sometimes troubled by predatory young women. After all, he is attractive as well as wealthy—'

'Estelle!' The Duque sounded furious. 'Leave it!'

Estelle shrugged, and gave Juliet a glance which said: *I told you so*, and Juliet bent her head.

'So, *senhorita*,' continued the Duque. 'Do go on.'

Juliet looked up. 'Well, I suggested that Teresa should be encouraged to go out – to swim – to attempt to do things for herself. I do not consider exercises, practised daily, adequate compensation for perhaps a swimming lesson – or more active pursuits.'

'Don't let her interfere, Tio Felipe,' exclaimed Teresa hotly. 'I don't want to do what she says. Can't I just live my life as I want to do?'

Juliet felt impatient. 'It seems to me, *senhor*, that your niece does not want to get better – to be able to walk again. That she enjoys spending her days in a wheelchair, arousing sympathy!'

'Senhorita Summers!' The Duque stubbed out his cheroot angrily. 'I will not have you suggest such a thing!'

Juliet compressed her lips. 'I'm sorry, *senhor*. Excuse me. I need – a wash before lunch!'

He did not attempt to detain her, but she was conscious of his eyes on her as she walked across the patio and into the *quinta*.

As she showered and changed, her altercation with

the Duque having produced a film of perspiration all over her body, her mind pondered on what she had said, and the more she pondered, the more she became convinced that she was right.

Teresa was not stupid. On the contrary, where getting what she wanted was concerned, Juliet thought she could be very bright, so what if she considered that her presence on the island was only tolerated because of her condition? If this were so, she might think that if she was cured the Duque would send her away. Surely, such ideas were sufficient to maintain the blockage which was causing her physical condition. The Duque had said it was a mental thing, had he not?

Juliet sighed. It would be her prerogative therefore to convince Teresa that her life was too important to spend it in a wheelchair. It would be no easy task. Teresa did not like her, and would fight her every inch of the way, using her own particular influence with the Duque to place her in the wrong if she could. And there was Nurse Madison, who would not help her at all, and who would, if she could, cause even more antipathy between her patient and her patient's new and annoying companion.

Emerging from the bathroom, Juliet dressed in a slim-fitting tunic of lemon cotton, smoothed her hair, and applied a coral lipstick to her lips.

Had she merely exchanged one disturbing situation for another? She frowned at her reflection in the mirror of her dressing table. Why was it then that whereas one situation had left her unhappy and dejected, the other aroused a sense of challenge, of purpose, inside her, so that she could not quell the rising feeling of excitement it engendered?

Calm down, she told herself, with emphasis. Work at it, but don't get involved! That would be fatal!

CHAPTER FOUR

IT seemed apparent that as Teresa's companion Juliet was expected to eat with the family. There were four for lunch, the Duque, Estelle Vinceiro, Teresa and herself. Estelle domineered the conversation, discussing friends they both had on the island, the price of sugar when the current crop was harvested, and the finds of a skin-diving expedition the Duque had joined.

The skin-diving expedition interested Juliet most. On holiday with her father she had made tentative dives with an instructor, but the stereotyped diving areas used by the instructors were not Juliet's idea of exciting. She was interested when the Duque mentioned the possibilities of there being a submerged wreck lying off the reef on the other side of the island. After all, the Caribbean thrived on tales of Spanish galleons, doubloons, and pieces of eight. When the Duque encountered her enquiring gaze, he said:

'You find treasure hunting exciting, *senhorita*?'

Juliet could not restrain her enthusiasm. 'Oh, yes, *senhor*. Doesn't everybody?' She replaced her wine glass on the gleaming damask of the tablecloth. 'Do you do much skin-diving?'

Estelle intervened, giving Juliet a rather thoughtful glance. 'The Duque does not have much time for trivial pursuits,' she remarked.

The Duque shrugged his broad shoulders, pouring

more wine into his own glass. 'What Senhora Vinceiro means is that *she* does not consider the search for the actual proof of history interesting,' he remarked surprisingly, and Juliet saw the annoyance in Estelle Vinceiro's eyes.

'You know perfectly well that skin-diving is a dangerous pastime,' she exclaimed. 'Your position here should invoke some sense of responsibility inside you!'

'I am absolutely aware of my responsibilities, Estelle,' returned the Duque smoothly, 'and skin-diving is only dangerous to the amateur!'

Juliet deemed it best to say no more, not wanting at all to cause any resentment from Estelle Vinceiro. She was her only ally to date. However, the Duque himself changed the subject and she was relieved.

When lunch was over, Teresa was taken away by Nurse Madison for her rest, and Juliet, feeling *de trop*, excused herself. But she could not help wondering what the Duque and Senhora Vinceiro intended to do, and couldn't understand the vague feeling of unrest she felt.

As it happened, Juliet saw no more of Teresa that day. At dinner, which she ate alone, the Duque dining out again, she was told that the young Senhorita had developed a headache and was dining in her room. Juliet doubted the authenticity of this information, but there was nothing she could do about it short of calling Teresa a liar.

After dinner, despite the desire to go down to the

beach, she returned to her room and tried to concentrate on the paperback novel she had brought with her. But its characters were cardboard people without warmth, or depth, and the life she was leading here, and the characters of the people she had encountered, were so much more interesting that at last she put it aside, and merely sat on her balcony in the dusk, watching the dipping lights of the yacht out in the bay.

The next morning, Teresa appeared at breakfast time, much to Juliet's relief. She had no desire to have to approach the Duque with a view to his speaking to his niece because she was incapable of handling her. Nurse Madison was with her, and Juliet thought Teresa had brought the nurse along for reinforcement.

Wishing them both good morning, she ordered rolls and coffee from the maid, and then smiled in what she hoped was a friendly way.

Teresa merely looked away, and Juliet realized she was as yet no further forward.

'I think we'll go on the beach this morning, Teresa,' she said brightly, waiting for the explosion.

Teresa sniffed. 'I think my uncle has other plans for me,' she returned smugly.

Juliet frowned. 'Oh! In what way?'

Teresa shrugged. 'He's taking me out with him, *senhorita*. So you will have to entertain yourself.'

She lay back in her wheelchair defiantly. Dressed in a cream dress with red embroidery, she looked young and attractive, and extremely satisfied with herself. Juliet wondered what the Duque was planning now.

By taking Teresa out with him, alone, he was encouraging her already active imagination to create situations and circumstances that were simply ridiculous. She felt impatient, and ate her breakfast in silence, conscious of Nurse Madison's mocking amusement all the while.

When a shadow fell across the little group, Juliet did not immediately look up, but continued to eat her meal despite the fact that she was conscious of the presence of the Duque with every fibre of her being.

'So, *senhorita*!' he remarked. 'I trust you slept well.'

Juliet was forced to look up now, registering everything about the man in that first moment. In a mustard silk shirt, dark brown riding breeches thrust into highly polished boots, the colour of his hair turning blue-black in the sunlight, he looked powerful and assured and very disturbing. He had rolled back the sleeves of his shirt, revealing muscular forearms dark with hairs, while the band of a gold watch encircled his wrist. With his shirt unbuttoned at the neckline, Juliet felt angrily assured that he was perfectly aware of his attraction, and the anger she had felt earlier was intensified by her own sensual weakness.

'I slept very well, thank you, *senhor*,' she replied, as evenly as she could, and returned her attention to her meal.

The Duque spoke to Nurse Madison, questioning her about Teresa's progress, and then speaking to Teresa herself. Juliet heard the caressing tone in Teresa's voice as she answered, and felt impotent to do anything about it with the Duque thwarting her every move.

But now the Duque had returned his attention to herself, and said: 'Has Teresa told you we are going out this morning, Senhorita Summers?'

Juliet lifted her eyes. 'Yes, *senhor*. I had intended taking Teresa on the beach today, but now, of course, that has had to be cancelled.'

She was aware of Teresa's angry eyes upon her, aware of the almost biting tone of her own voice which was not altogether to do with her young charge, but could do nothing about it.

The Duque ran a hand over the thickness of his hair. Combed across his head from a low side parting, it persisted in lying across his forehead, and he brushed it back only to have it spring forward again immediately. His dark eyes were enigmatic as he said:

'Surely Teresa explained that your presence is also required.'

Juliet's eyes darted to Teresa, registering the girl's anger, and Nurse Madison's astonishment. Obviously Teresa had omitted to tell Nurse Madison this also.

'Your – niece only said that she was accompanying you,' said Juliet now, unable in the circumstances to evade the question.

'I see.' The Duque looked at Teresa. 'Why was that, Teresa?'

Teresa wrinkled her nose. 'Senhorita Summers jumps to conclusions, Tio Felipe. I didn't say she was not coming.'

Juliet could have denied this, but as she knew, and

Teresa knew, she did not think it worth the trouble.

'Might – might I ask where we are going?' Juliet asked.

The Duque drew out his cheroots. 'I have to go to Venterra, the village you saw on your arrival, *senhorita*. My business there will not take long, and afterwards I thought we might drive over to Lauganca Bay on the far side of the island. It is the area reported to have seen the destruction of several Spanish galleons. I thought the area might interest you, *senhorita*.'

Juliet was astounded and looked it. Gathering her wits, she said: 'Might we go on to the beach, *senhor*?'

Teresa stiffened at once, giving Juliet an incensed look when the Duque said: 'I do not see why not, do you, Nurse Madison?'

Nurse Madison shrugged indifferently, obviously put out. 'You make the decisions here, Senhor Duque.'

The Duque gave her a wry glance and then allowed his gaze to flicker over Juliet's slim-fitting dress. 'Are you ready now, Senhorita Summers?'

Juliet hesitated. 'Give me a minute, *senhor*,' she said quickly, swallowing the remains of her coffee.

Dashing up to her room, she swiftly slid off the dress she had been wearing, and pulled on cotton pants in a particularly attractive shade of apple green and a lace overblouse of pink Tricel. Then she opened a drawer and extracted two bathing suits; one in navy blue trimmed with white, and the other in emerald green. She doubted that she would need them, but if the

71

opportunity arose she did not want Teresa to say that she had no swimsuit. After retrieving a basket-type shopper from the bottom of the wardrobe, she put the suits inside together with towels and a pair of dark glasses. Satisfied that she would do, she ran back down the stairs to the hall.

Neither Teresa nor the Duque were around, but when she looked out of the lounge windows she saw a sleek convertible parked on the forecourt, waiting for its occupants.

Frowning, she walked slowly out to the car, and looked around. It was a beautiful morning, although there were clouds in the sky, and she thought there might be showers later. She could see the gardeners working among the trees, singing at their tasks, and felt a sense of wellbeing which was shattered when she turned and saw the Duque walking towards her carrying a triumphant-looking Teresa in his arms.

Juliet turned away. It was such a difficult situation, she thought with a heavy sigh. By trying to show the Duque that Teresa was very susceptible to his charms, she was destroying her own defences against possible counter-attack. Teresa might just as easily imagine she, Juliet, was jealous of the Duque's attentions. Oh, it was ridiculous, thought Juliet impatiently. Couldn't the man see what he was encouraging? Of course, Teresa was helpless, at least no one could prove otherwise but Teresa herself, and she had to be carried when she was not in her wheelchair, but did it have to be the Duque who carried her? Actually, in normal circumstances, it would have been the most natural thing, but these were not *normal* circumstances.

She heard the Duque's footsteps behind her, and swung round to encounter Teresa's satisfied expression. Schooling herself not to show her annoyance, she was therefore unprepared for the Duque's first words:

'Teresa did not wish to bring the wheelchair after all. It is collapsible, *senhorita*, and at first that was our intention. However, after I had dismissed Miguel, she changed her mind again.'

Juliet looked into his dark eyes, but they were completely expressionless, except that she could sense, rather than see, a kind of suppressed amusement, as though he had known all along what she was thinking.

He had answered her unspoken question, he had removed the reason for her impatience, why then did she feel so furiously angry with him?

'Please, get in the car, *senhorita*,' he murmured lazily, and deciding there was little to be achieved, standing there, staring at him like some stupid schoolgirl, she slid into the back of the car. The Duque put Teresa into the front seat, beside his own, and then walked round to climb in beside her. He gave Juliet a cursory glance before setting the car in motion, but Juliet had the feeling that in spite of her antagonism towards him she didn't exist for him as a woman but merely as someone, with radical ideas, who just happened to be Teresa's companion. After all, Estelle Vinceiro left little to the imagination, and it was obvious that she considered the Duque her property. And maybe he was, and what of it? thought Juliet, crossly.

They drove away from the *quinta* in the opposite direction from that taken by Juliet the previous morning, and unable to suppress her interest, Juliet leaned forward in her seat, watching everything with heightened intensity.

The Duque drove fast, but expertly, the car making swift progress towards Venterra. They passed dark-skinned islanders along the road, men working in the sugar cane fields, or tending the bean plantations, women with young children, some riding on their backs, making their way to the market in Venterra; and all acknowledged the Duque's car, showing more clearly than words how liked and respected the aristocratic lord of Venterra really was. The colours were an assault on the eyes, and the scents and fragrances were an assault on the senses. Juliet didn't know how anyone could live on Venterra without being completely aware of its atmosphere. She had visited the West Indies before, so why was everything so much more brilliant, colourful and exciting this time? She refused to try and solve that particular problem. She was merely unsophisticated and over-sensitive, or so she told herself.

The Duque parked the car on the quay, leaving the two girls alone while he went into a warehouse to see about the importation of certain items he required which would be arriving on the island steamer that afternoon. Tall and dark, despite his tanned complexion, he stood out among the dark-skinned West

Indians, exchanging a word here and there, inclining his head to listen to someone's problem; he was everything an island despot should be, thought Juliet ruefully, taking out her cigarettes, and lighting one as she viewed the bustling scene before her.

Obviously, all the commerce of the island was conducted here, and there were stalls selling fish and meat, fruit and vegetables, as well as materials and cooking utensils. There was the smell of fish and drying ropes, the musky smell of soft fruit and the inescapable scent of humanity. It was strong, and not always pleasant, and yet it blended with the swaying hips and basket-adorned heads of the West Indians, to whom rhythm and music was everything. Even at this hour a steel band was practising somewhere, while a boy sat on the stone jetty strumming a guitar.

And over it all beamed the sun, like a benevolent uncle.

Juliet sighed, and Teresa turned to look at her. 'We've never discussed it, Senhorita Summers, but how did you persuade my uncle that your presence here was warranted?' Her eyes were cold and calculating.

Juliet felt momentarily at a disadvantage, and then, as though recalling that Teresa was much younger than she was, she said coolly: 'As you're so fond of intrigue, Teresa, why don't you ask your uncle yourself?'

Teresa's colour deepened. 'Don't be clever, *senhorita*. You're only here on sufferance, remember that!' She pouted her lips. 'I am glad I do not have to work for my living. It must be awful feeling inferior all the time.'

Juliet studied the tip of her cigarette. 'Why should *I* feel inferior, Teresa?' she asked.

Teresa gave a derisive sneer. 'Well, it's obvious, isn't it? I mean – this island – the *quinta* – must be vastly different from anything you're used to.'

'So?' Juliet's eyes were holding Teresa's.

'So you're just – just a *servant*!'

'And all servants are inferior, is that it?'

Teresa shrugged.

Juliet compressed her lips for a moment. 'Then let me tell you something, Teresa; there are rich and poor in this life, but what you are, or what you achieve, or simply what you do, is not designated by wealth and its compensations. A person has to find more than *things* to live with. Most of all a person has to live with himself. I sometimes wonder if you've ever found it difficult to live with yourself!'

'*Porco!* How dare you speak to me like that!' Teresa's face was incensed.

Juliet shrugged, and lay back in her seat. 'Don't imagine you can continually criticize me without getting something in return,' she replied softly. 'There are lengths to everyone's patience!'

Teresa was breathing swiftly with anger, chewing furiously at her lips. Obviously, since coming to the island, no one, apart perhaps from Estelle Vinceiro, had ever crossed her.

At last she said: 'Felipe listens to me. I shall speak to him. I shall find out what lies you have told him about me!'

'Lies!' exclaimed Juliet. 'What lies?'

'The lies you must have invented to make him let you stay here.' Teresa calmed herself a little. 'Yes. We will see who can win in this game, *senhorita.*'

Juliet half-smiled. Teresa was so young. Even her malevolence was a childish thing. Why then did she harbour such adult ideas about the Duque?

'All right,' she said, shrugging. 'You play the game, Teresa, and maybe we will all be surprised at the outcome.'

They were sitting in stony silence when the Duque returned, and he frowned as he got into the driving seat. 'The atmosphere in this car could be cut with a knife,' he remarked thoughtfully. 'Might I ask why?'

Teresa adopted the offended air she usually used in his presence. 'Senhorita Summers has been very rude to me,' she said, bending her head, in an appealing manner. 'Tio Felipe, surely you can see that all Senhorita Summers does is frighten and upset me.'

'Frighten?' The Duque set the car in motion, turning through the village square. 'You are exaggerating, Teresa.'

Teresa gave him a deliberately hurt look. 'No – no, I'm not. Yesterday – yesterday you didn't ask where we drove. Oh, even to think about it.' She covered her eyes with her hands. 'I – I was terrified. I – I wasn't going to tell you – to worry you, but now I must!'

Juliet raised her eyes heavenward. She was absolutely sure that the reason Teresa had not mentioned their journey yesterday sooner was because when she had seen Estelle Vinceiro with the Duque all thoughts of anything else had gone out of her head, and anything that was so easily banished could not have been as frightening as she was now making out.

The Duque lit a cheroot, while negotiating a bend that took them higher up the slopes above the sea, and curved round a promontory ahead leading to the far side of the island.

'Well,' he said. 'Where did you go?' He glanced round at Juliet. 'As my niece appears to be overcome, can you tell me, *senhorita*?'

'Yes,' replied Juliet easily. 'We drove up to a place called Venterra Montanah.'

'Venterra Montanah!' The Duque swung the car round a curve and came to a halt. '*Venterra Montañah!* Teresa, is this so?'

Juliet hunched her shoulders. 'Did I say something wrong?' she asked, with some sarcasm.

The Duque swung round in his seat, his dark eyes accusing. 'Are you aware of the dangers of that road?'

'Dangers? You mean the curves?'

'Yes, *senhorita*, I mean the curves!' The Duque looked furious.

Juliet sighed. 'Well, for heaven's sake, I've driven on roads with much worse curves and gradients than those!' As soon as she said the words she wished she hadn't, for immediately the Duque looked sceptical.

'Indeed,' he said slowly. 'And where, might I ask, have you driven on worse roads than those?'

Even Teresa had taken away her hands from her

eyes and was looking curiously at her new companion.

Juliet shrugged deciding there was no use in making anything up. 'In the Alps, *senhor*, the Swiss Alps!'

'I see. You have driven in the Swiss Alps.'

'Yes, *senhor*.'

'And might one ask how a girl who reputedly has to work for a living comes to be driving in the Swiss Alps?'

Juliet had had a moment to think about this. 'I – I was companion-chauffeuse to an elderly – lady,' she said smoothly. 'We went to Monte Carlo last year.'

'Is that so?' The Duque studied her intently. Then he looked at Teresa, and finally back at Juliet, almost reading her thoughts, she felt, with his penetrating gaze. 'Very well, *senhorita*. I will take your word for it. Nevertheless, Venterra Montanah is not for the amateur. I would rather you chose other routes for your outings. Teresa, obviously your fears were not based in reality. Maybe your emotional condition accounted for your fears.'

Teresa could not let it go so easily. She was not to be thwarted. 'You – you weren't there, Tio Felipe! You are taking her word for everything! She drove carelessly, I tell you. I was terrified!'

Juliet gasped. 'Teresa, that's not true!'

'It is so. I don't believe you've ever driven on roads in the Alps. I think you're telling my uncle lies!'

Juliet felt angry now. Earlier she had been exasperated, and then amused, but now she was really angry. Teresa seemed to think she had no defence against this man who was her employer.

Leaning forward, keeping her voice light and provocative, she said: '*Senhor*, your niece seems determined to put me in the wrong. In order to prove my point, would you allow me to drive *you* up to Venterra Montanah?'

Teresa eyes widened, and the Duque looked impatient.

'That is not necessary, *senhorita*. I am quite prepared to accept—'

'But I am not,' insisted Juliet, her eyes mocking. 'At least allow me to prove my case, or I shall think you are unfairly biased in your niece's favour.'

The Duque lifted his shoulders. '*Senhorita*, I have told you I believe you.'

'Are you afraid also, *senhor*.' Juliet didn't quite know why she said that. Certainly it was not to prove anything to Teresa. Maybe it was to prove something to herself.

His eyes darkened momentarily, and something stirred in their depths, something that brought the hot colour surging to Juliet's cheeks.

'No, *senhorita*,' he murmured, 'I am not afraid.' He drew on his cheroot. 'And some time I will accept your challenge, and allow you to drive me to Venterra Montanah, *sim*?' He looked at Teresa. 'Does that satisfy you, *pequena*?'

Teresa looked furious, and Juliet couldn't dispel the feeling of having trodden too far into strange territory. Challenging the Duque in an attempt to bait Teresa was one thing, but challenging him because she wanted to challenge him was quite another. Her experience of men was not so great; naturally in her position as Robert Lindsay's daughter, she had had plenty of boyfriends, and she was not unaware of the facts of life. But they had been young men, most of them as unversed in the arts of sexual encounter as she was herself; her father had seen to that. She had not been allowed to run around with the so-called jet set, or to attend parties which could only be classed as doubtful.

The Duque was an entirely unknown quantity. He was no boy, he was a man, and the sensations he aroused inside her were completely outside her previous experience.

As the car moved on, Juliet attempted to retrieve her nonchalance, without a great deal of success. So she studied the scenery instead, trying to distinguish the various plants and flowers that grew in such profusion. It was no use worrying about something that quite possibly would never happen.

Lauganca Bay was unbelievably beautiful. Larger than the other coves Juliet had seen, it stretched for miles, white sand, green water and grey rocks. When the Duque brought the car to a halt, she slid out without waiting for permission, and walked across the headland, looking across the wide expanse of water which had once seen the demise of so many Spanish hopes. With the swirling waters high there was little to show the dangerous rock formations that lay just below the surface, like the smooth face of a lake that guarded undercurrents of disaster.

Juliet sighed and then turned back to the car, rubbing her elbows with the palms of her hands. The Duque and Teresa were still sitting in the car, and Juliet was suddenly conscious of the slim-fitting slacks and sleeveless overblouse. Her hair had blown in strands from the braids, and she felt sure she must look an absolute sight.

At her approach the Duque slid out of the car, standing tall and powerful in front of her.

'So, *senhorita*,' he murmured, 'what do you think?'

Juliet flushed. 'It's very beautiful,' she replied swiftly. 'Can – can we go down?'

'I don't see why not. I can bring Teresa.'

'Yes.' Juliet brushed past him and lifted her basket bag out of the rear of the car, aware of that awful twisted feeling in her stomach again. Get a hold of yourself, she told herself angrily. You only met him two days ago. What are you thinking of?

They descended to the beach by way of a sloping path that ran down the steep incline. The sand was soft at the rim, damp nearer the water, showing how the tide could cover the ground.

The Duque put Teresa down on a rug he had brought from the car, and then said: 'See – the motor boat we use for our expeditions – it is housed in the boathouse there.'

Juliet saw a wooden building at the far end of the beach, near the rocky headland. She nodded, wishing she knew more about skin-diving. Discussing the kind of dives she had made with the Duque would not arouse any interest on his part. Merely a surfeit of questions as to how she had any knowledge at all.

Teresa heaved a sigh. 'Must we stay here long, Tio Felipe?' she asked impatiently. 'The sun is hot, and I am thirsty.'

The Duque smiled down at her. 'Are you being a little awkward, *pequena*?' he countered. 'Perhaps Senhorita Summers would like to swim.'

Juliet shook her head. The idea of appearing before the Duque in a bathing suit was a daunting one which she had not really considered before. 'Thank you, but no,' she replied, sitting down on the sand beside Teresa.

The Duque nodded to her basket. 'I had thought you brought swimming equipment,' he remarked. 'It is early yet. I have some coffee in a flask in the car. There is no reason why we should not stay here for a while.'

Juliet didn't know whether he was baiting her now or not. She only knew she couldn't do it.

'Will you be swimming, *senhor*?' she asked, studying her nails.

Teresa stared at her, and then at her uncle, but the Duque was not disturbed. 'No, *senhorita*. Unlike you, I am not prepared. However, if Teresa will sit here for a while, and have some coffee, I will take you to the boathouse and show you some of our equipment.'

Juliet felt Teresa stiffen with anger. 'Tio Felipe, I cannot stay here on the sand alone!'

'Why not?' The Duque left them, mounting the cliff path with ease, to get the flask of coffee from the car.

Teresa gave Juliet an angry stare. 'So, *senhorita*, you think you have won.'

Juliet sighed. 'It's not a battle, Teresa. For heaven's sake, why can't you just accept my company? I'm not trying to hurt you. I want to help you!'

'I don't need any help!'

'Well, I think you do.' Juliet rose to her feet. 'Don't you want to walk again?'

'Of course I do,' Teresa exclaimed.

'Well then, try and see that by using your limbs you will regain the power over them!'

'How?'

'Swimming!'

'No, thanks.' Teresa glanced round and saw the Duque descending the path again. 'You're just like Laura Weston, do you know that?'

'The other companion?'

'Yes. I'll bet my uncle did not tell you why she was dismissed.'

'He said you didn't like her.'

'No, I didn't.' Teresa sneered. 'But that wasn't why she was dismissed.' She put the tips of her fingers together. 'She made a fool of herself over Felipe, that's why she was dismissed!'

Juliet felt the colour wash over her body. 'Well,' she said, speaking quickly before the Duque arrived, 'you need have no anxiety in that direction, so far as I am concerned.'

'No?'

'No.'

The Duque reached them. 'There you are, Teresa,' he said, smiling. 'Some coffee, and some dark glasses. We won't be very long.'

Teresa shrugged, apparently accepting the situation, but Juliet wondered whether her mind was already pondering possibilities of her new companion making a fool of herself over her uncle, and thus bringing about her own dismissal.

In consequence, as they walked across the sand together, Juliet felt tongue-tied, and the Duque studied her expression thoughtfully.

'I am quite aware of my niece's facility for causing dissension,' he remarked surprisingly. 'Teresa is young and painfully aware of her vulnerability. Maybe that is why she clings to me.'

Juliet shrugged, not answering, and he said, a little impatiently: '*Senhorita*, at the risk of appearing conceited, I must confess you do not appear to enjoy my company as much as any other woman of my acquaintance.'

Juliet stared at him now, her cheeks burning. 'I am sorry, *senhor*. I was thinking of other things.'

'Obviously. Might one ask what "things"?'

She sighed. 'You didn't tell me Miss Weston was dismissed because she became — well, infatuated with you.'

He smiled now, completely without mockery, and Juliet was struck again by the magnetic appeal he emanated. '*Deus*,' he exclaimed, 'you are the most forthright young woman I have ever met. You do not — how do you say — pull your punches; do you?'

'Is it true?'

He shrugged. 'Maybe.'

'In other words — yes.'

85

He did not reply, and then they reached the boat-house, and he extracted a bunch of keys from the pocket of his riding breeches, and inserted one in the lock.

Inside, it was gloomy and a little damp-smelling, as though the wood might be rotting in places. There was a sleek motor boat, painted red and white, lying in the centre, and along the sides of the building were hung rubber diving suits, oxygen cylinders, masks and goggles, and all the other paraphernalia common to skin-diving.

Leaving the door wide to admit the light, the Duque showed Juliet how the cylinders worked, and she had to appear completely ignorant of the technicalities.

The Duque climbed into the motor boat, examining the fuel gauge, turning on the ignition, doing all the usual checks a boatman might do. He went down on his haunches, climbing into the small covered cabin of the craft, while Juliet interested herself in a map she had found hanging on the wall. When the Duque emerged again, swinging up on to the wooden planking, several of the buttons of his shirt had become loosened, leaving his chest bare to his waist, darkly tanned, and covered with dark hairs. He walked past Juliet, wiped his hands on a cloth, and said:

'I see you are examining the chart. The crosses mark the dives that have already been made.' He came to stand beside her, but that was too much for Juliet. There was something wholly disturbing about his almost animal sensuality, and her own emotions were rapidly disturbing her.

With jerky movements, she brushed past him, intending to get out into the sunshine as soon as was possible, but her foot slipped on the planks, her ankle turned, and she stumbled and would have fallen had he not caught her, grasping her arms, and pulling her up so that momentarily she was against the hard warmth of his chest. She felt the smoothness of his skin with its overlying layer of hair beneath her fingers, and knew that she wanted to slide her arms round his neck, and put her mouth against the firm lips of the Duque. Everything Teresa had said swam dizzily through her mind, and with a wrench she was out of his arms and out of the boathouse with superhuman speed.

CHAPTER FIVE

The journey back to the *quinta* was uneventful. Only Teresa seemed aware that something was amiss, and her eyes had narrowed curiously at Juliet's sudden return to her on the beach, minus the Duque. He came a little while later, strolling lazily across the sand after locking up the boathouse again. He spoke to Teresa, relaxed with her, and completely ignored Juliet.

After lunch, which was a silent meal, the Duque excused himself, Teresa was taken by Nurse Madison for her rest, and Juliet was left to her own devices. She decided to stay in her own room, and read a little before lying down and allowing her thoughts free rein.

She determinedly thrust all thoughts of Duque Felipe de Castro out of her mind, and thought instead about Rosemary, and her father. She wondered whether he had made any progress in endeavouring to find her. It seemed much more than six days since she left England. The life there, her friends and activities, seemed a world away. A world moreover to which she had no desire to return. That was the frightening thing. Whereas in the beginning, it had begun almost as an escapade, now it had achieved the proportions of something large and important, and she no longer wanted to jeopardize her chances of remaining on Venterra, even if it meant humouring Teresa.

In this, of course, she was helped by Estelle Vinceiro's attitude, and also that of the Duque himself.

The Duque!

Her thoughts raced. What had happened in the boathouse that morning? Had he been aware of her nervousness, of the primitive sensations he aroused in her? Had he sensed her controlled withdrawal had been brought about by a supreme test of will-power?

She rolled on to her stomach, recalling the feel of his body against hers. She had never felt that way before. She had swum with boys, kissed boys in bathing suits, so why did the Duque disturb her so much? She had always criticized girls who allowed their emotions to rule their heads. She had always thought they were foolish and weak-willed. But now she was beginning to feel the strength of an attraction that cared little for will-power, or convention. After all, the Duque was much older than she was, and obviously more experienced. Who could say but that maybe he had indulged in a light affair with this girl, Laura Weston, and then after her dismissal had pretended she had been the guilty party! Maybe he indulged in affairs often. Maybe, as she was young, and a new face around the *quinta*, he thought she might enjoy it too.

Then she squashed these ideas. Whatever else the Duque might be he was not promiscuous. She didn't know exactly how she knew this, but she did. A man who lived life lightly, uncaring of a person's feelings, could not inspire such love and devotion in his people as she had witnessed in Venterra that morning.

She rolled on to her back again. It was ridiculous really, she thought, sighing. Even indulging in this kind of mental pondering. After all, sooner or later Robert Lindsay would find her, and then . . .

The Duque had visitors for dinner that evening, so Juliet asked Consuelo if she could have her dinner in her room. It seemed apparent that Nurse Madison intended keeping Teresa with her for the remainder of the afternoon when her siesta was over, so that Juliet's involvement with the girl was very slight. Apart from the morning, she was obviously going to be left to herself, and she had no desire to intrude on any dinner party the Duque might be giving. Consuelo had told her that there were to be six for dinner: Estelle Vinceiro; the Duque's sister Amalia and her husband, Juan Bestado; a young Spaniard called Francisco Valmos, as well as Teresa and the Duque himself.

The next morning, she breakfasted with Teresa as usual, and then had Miguel assist her to persuade the girl to go in the car. They drove to Venterra, and Teresa stayed moodily in the car while Juliet did some personal shopping. She had offered to assist the girl into her wheelchair, but she wouldn't listen to her, and in consequence Juliet felt guilty again.

The Duque was not present for lunch, and Consuelo said: 'Your uncle asked me to give you a message, *senhorita*.'

Teresa looked more alert than she had done all morning. 'Yes?'

'He has had to fly to Barbados on business, and may not be back for a few days, *senhorita*. Apparently it was a sudden decision, brought about by a telephone call

90

this morning.'

Teresa looked sullen. 'Oh, really!' She chewed at her lip angrily. 'Is that all?'

'I think so, *senhorita*. If you had been at home at the time—'

'Of course. *If!*' muttered Teresa, with passion. She looked at Juliet. 'I suppose you imagine this will give you the chance to treat me as you like.'

Juliet gasped. 'Of course not!'

'It is as well, for you will be disappointed!' said Teresa harshly.

Juliet gave a sigh. 'Why must you persist in this ridiculous antagonism?' she exclaimed wearily. 'Can't you see I'm here now, and there's nothing you can do about it!'

'Isn't there? Isn't there just!' Teresa wheeled her chair away from the table. 'Consuelo! Get Nurse Madison. I want to go to my room.'

Teresa's rooms, Juliet knew, were on the ground floor for convenience, but as she had never been invited there, she didn't know where they were.

Leaving the table herself, she walked outside on to the patio, wishing Teresa was a simple ordinary girl, with ordinary tastes, and ordinary likes and dislikes, not ruled by an obsessive passion for her uncle.

With decision, she went up to her room, donned her black swimsuit, and throwing a striped black and white towelling beach coat over all, she descended the stairs again, and crossed the gardens to the path leading down to the beach.

Shading her eyes with dark glasses, she sunbathed

for a while before plunging into the cooling waters of the Caribbean. Although the water was warm, it was refreshing, and she swam lazily, turning on to her back and floating.

Afterwards she lay on the beach again, and then returned to the *quinta* in time for afternoon tea, which was invariably served in her room. However, today as she crossed the marble hall, Estelle Vinceiro appeared from the direction of the lounge, and said:

'Excuse me, Senhorita Summers. Have you a moment? Will you have tea with me?'

Juliet smiled. 'Well, if you will allow me to dress first,' she exclaimed ruefully.

Estelle inclined her small, delicately moulded head. 'Of course. I shall await you in the lounge.'

The lounge was a large but comfortable room, well endowed with deep armchairs and settees, its elegance coming from an intricately carved ceiling and tapestry-hung walls. A superb collection of china and porcelain were in a large cabinet, and there was a chiming French clock on the mantel above a magnificent fireplace.

When Juliet returned, feeling more relaxed in a slim-fitting white shift of embroidered cotton, she found Estelle sitting on a skin-covered couch, in command of a silver tea service and wafer thin cups and saucers.

'Cream and sugar, *senhorita*?' she questioned.

'Just cream, thank you,' said Juliet, sitting down opposite her. 'It's a beautiful day.'

'Yes, isn't it? There you are!' She handed Juliet a

cup of tea, offered sandwiches and cakes, and then taking her own cup, lay back lazily, crossing her legs, for all the world as though she were already mistress of the *quinta*.

Juliet sipped her tea, thinking desperately of something to say. 'The – er – Duque left this morning for Barbados,' she ventured.

Estelle smiled silkily. 'Yes, I know. Naturally, he telephoned me before his departure.'

Juliet smiled, nodded, returned her attention to her tea. Estelle was scrutinizing her very thoroughly, and although she liked the woman, she did not like such appraising scrutiny.

Finally, Estelle said: 'Tell me, *senhorita*, how are you getting on with Teresa?'

Juliet sighed. She did not want to offend the other woman but nor did she particularly want to discuss Teresa with her.

'We – we are making – slow progress,' she said awkwardly.

'That I can believe. And the Duque? Does he take Teresa's part so that your job is doubly difficult?'

'No. That is – I don't think so.'

Estelle nodded, as though well satisfied. 'You may not know, Senhorita Summers, but at the time Teresa's accident occurred, Felipe – that is, the Duque and I, were planning to get married.'

Juliet stiffened. 'Oh, yes?'

'Yes. That is why, naturally, I am endeavouring to find someone to whom Teresa will take a liking. It is difficult, you understand. Felipe will not consider marriage while Teresa is so helpless – so dependent upon him.'

'I see.' Juliet finished her tea and stood down her cup. Estelle flicked open a cigarette box on the table, and said:

'Do you smoke, *senhorita*?'

Juliet said she did, took a cigarette, and accepted a light. Estelle did not smoke, but folded her hands, and continued to survey her companion.

'Do you not have a boy-friend, *senhorita*? Someone at home, in England, someone special?'

Juliet shook her head. 'I'm afraid not.'

'That is sad. You are – how old?'

'Twenty-one, *senhora*.'

'Hmm. It is surprising. You are an attractive girl. Are your parents alive?'

'Only my father, *senhora*.'

'Your mother is dead?'

'She died when I was born.'

Juliet was getting a little tired of this catechism. There were plenty of questions she would have liked to ask, but she doubted whether she would get answers for them.

The Senhora seemed to realize this, for she said: 'I am sorry if I appear curious, *senhorita*, but as Teresa's – well – aunt-to-be, I feel a little responsible.'

'I see.'

'Please don't be offended.' Estelle smiled, and Juliet allowed herself to smile also, although a little of her liking for Senhora Vinceiro was evaporating. Her possessive attitude was rather annoying. and the way she acted as though she was already in charge was bound to infuriate Teresa if it annoyed Juliet. For all her friendliness, Juliet felt that Estelle was merely using her and that her friendliness was just a way of getting what she wanted. Maybe she thought that in Juliet she had an ally in her effort to get the Duque to agree to a marriage in the near future. What she couldn't know was the emotional chaos Juliet herself had been plunged into since her arrival on Venterra.

She even felt a sneaking sympathy for Teresa, and her unrewarding infatuation for the man who had brought her here. There was so much to like and admire about the Duque that it would not be difficult to fall in love with him.

Fall in love with him!

Juliet brought herself up short. She was allowing her imagination to run away with her. Just because the Duque was something outside of her experience, outside of the normal run of men, that was no reason to mistake admiration for infatuation.

All of a sudden, she wanted to get away from Estelle Vinceiro and the disturbing thoughts she aroused. She had done enough thinking the previous day. She had no desire to think any more!

Standing up, she said: 'Will you excuse me, *senhora*? I – I have things I want to do. Letters to write. You understand?'

Estelle Vinceiro studied her for a moment longer, and then said: 'Of course, *senhorita*. But I would like to say that I hope we can be friends. In this – er – in the *quinta*, you will find plenty of antagonism. I would like to think that any troubles you encounter, you might bring to me.'

Juliet bit her lip. 'It's very kind of you to say so, but I don't think—'

'You can never tell!' interposed Estelle smoothly. '*Adeus*, for the moment.'

Juliet made her way to her room, on legs that were strangely weak. It must be the swimming, she thought, closing her bedroom door wearily. It must have tired me more than I imagined!

In the ten days that followed Juliet suffered a great deal of antagonism. To begin with, in her uncle's absence, Teresa refused to join her companion for breakfast, spending hours in her rooms with Nurse Madison. As each day passed, Juliet realized she had absolutely no control over the girl, and what was more she had no authority while the Duque was away.

It infuriated her, but there was little she could do, short of actually dragging Teresa out of her room, and as she didn't know where that room was, that prevented that. She could have questioned the servants, but it seemed such a menial way of going on, and she was not used to humiliating herself like this.

By the end of the first week that the Duque was away, Juliet was spending most of her time alone. She swam, she sunbathed, she even played tennis with Miguel, but she was bored, for this was what she had left England for. She had questioned Consuelo as to where she might get in touch with the Duque, but after an abortive series of telephone calls to hotels in Barbados, she gave up. She could see nothing for it but to wait until the Duque returned.

Then, one morning, she had a visitor. He was a tall, lean young Spaniard, and introduced himself as Francisco Valmos.

Juliet smiled, glad of anyone new to speak to. 'You must be the Señor Valmos who dined here a week ago,' she exclaimed.

He smiled. He was very handsome, and obviously rather bemused by Juliet's cool, auburn-haired beauty after the dark and dusky-skinned women of his own race.

'That is correct, *señorita*,' he agreed enthusiastically. 'But now I am told Felipe is away.'

'Yes. In Barbados.'

'Ah, that is unfortunate, but yet pleasing, for now I can speak to you without fear of interruption. My – er – distant cousin, Estelle Vinceiro, told me a little about you.'

'And she didn't tell you that Fel— the Duque was away?'

He looked a little shamefaced. 'Actually, yes, I knew. But I wanted to meet you for myself.'

Juliet laughed. 'Oh, really!' She folded her arms, looking at him mockingly. Francisco Valmos was a little like the young men she was used to. With him she would have no difficulties.

'Yes. So *señorita*, will you offer me some chocolate, and we can talk, here on the patio?'

'All right. Why not?' Juliet summoned Consuelo. 'Two chocolates, please, Consuelo.'

When they were seated on the patio, with their drinks, and cigarettes were lighted, Francisco said:

'Estelle did not exaggerate. You are quite beautiful, do you know that?'

Juliet wrinkled her nose. 'That is not necessary, *señor*.'

'Oh, please, call me Francisco. What may I call you?'

Juliet hesitated. 'Well, Rosemary is my name, but you can call me Juliet.'

'Juliet? Why?'

'I prefer it,' she replied, and then: 'Actually, I'm glad of someone to talk to. I haven't seen Teresa alone for more than two days.'

He frowned. 'Why? Is she being difficult?'

Juliet sighed. 'Is she ever anything else?'

He chuckled. 'Oh, yes. She can be charming. Teresa is a fair example of her race; she likes men. Do you want me to speak to her?'

'Would it do any good?'

'I don't know, I should think so. What exactly had you planned to do with Teresa?'

Juliet sighed. 'Many things. Just now, I think, if she would talk to me, I'd feel I'd achieved something!'

'It's that bad?'

'Yes,' Juliet nodded. 'Not much use, am I? I suppose when the Duque comes back I'll be dismissed too.'

Francisco sighed. 'Maybe – maybe not. At any rate, I'll speak to Teresa. How about all of us going on a picnic? Would you like that?'

'To the beach?'

'Yes. I have a bathing tent, if anybody is shy,' he grinned.

'It sounds ideal,' agreed Juliet, sighing. 'Oh, yes, Francisco. Will you try?'

Juliet never found out what Francisco said to Teresa, but within an hour they were all in Francisco's car, together with a picnic hamper which Consuelo had supplied, on their way to Francisco's parents' home to collect his own equipment.

For all Juliet's apprehensions, she had to concede that Francisco was marvellous with Teresa. She obviously liked him, and certainly she received plenty of attention. It was only when he suggested she put on the swim suit which Juliet had brought for her that she shied away, like a frightened horse.

Juliet left them arguing on the beach, and when she returned from her swim, they were still there. Francisco was attempting to persuade Teresa in their own language, or Teresa's language, at least, and Juliet lay on the sand, praying he would succeed. If she was to be dismissed, which thought absolutely terrified her, she would like to think she had achieved something towards Teresa's recovery, even if it was only an idea, and someone else did all the work.

At last even Francisco grew impatient, and left them both to have a swim himself. While he was in the water, Teresa said:

'Don't you imagine your presence here retrieves any of your lost progress! My uncle shall hear of the way you have played around since his departure. Nurse Madison and I will both be able to prove that!'

Juliet sighed. 'I really think there is something wrong with you, Teresa,' she exclaimed wearily. 'All you can think about is getting rid of me. Why? Do you think by doing so you will rid yourself of companions for all time? I can assure you, if I go, Estelle will get somebody else.'

Teresa looked surprised. 'What do you know about Estelle's ideas?'

'Just about everything,' replied Juliet, running her tongue over her lips. 'She intends to marry your uncle in the very near future, whether you're here or not. By remaining inanimate, which is what you are doing, you are giving all the advantages to her. Can't you see that?'

'Are you encouraging me to believe that my uncle might see me more clearly if I were walking?'

Juliet stiffened. 'No, I did not say that! My God, surely you can see that this – this infatuation you have for Felipe is ridiculous!'

Teresa's eyes darkened. '*Felipe!*' she echoed. 'Since when have you called my uncle Felipe?'

Juliet's cheeks burned. 'The – the Duque is not my concern,' she said, attempting to evade the question.

'Since when have you called the Duque Felipe?' hissed Teresa menacingly.

'Since no time. Never!' Juliet sat up, drawing up her knees and resting her chin on the top of them.

Teresa's fingers plucked her dress restlessly.

'I don't believe you. That day – that day you were with him in the boathouse – what happened?'

Juliet stared at her incredulously. 'What happened?

What happened?' Something inside her burst into incensed rage. 'I'll tell you what happened, Teresa. Your uncle made savage and passionate love to me! Now are you satisfied? Would you like the details? Would you like to know how many times he kissed me – how he caressed me? Did you notice that his shirt was unbuttoned? I did that!'

Teresa stared at her with eyes wide and disbelieving. 'Stop it! Stop it!' she cried wildly, putting her hands over her ears. 'I won't – I don't believe you!'

Juliet lifted her shoulders in a helpless gesture. 'Why not? It's what you wanted to hear, isn't it?'

'No. No. *No!*' Teresa's hands were balled into fists. 'Oh, I hate you, I hate you, *I hate you!*'

'I don't blame you,' said Juliet quietly, getting to her feet. 'That was a horrible thing to say, and I'm sorry.'

'You mean—' Teresa looked up at her. 'You mean – it's not true?'

'True? True? Of course it's not true! Do you think I would tell you, if it were?'

Teresa shook her head bewilderedly. 'But I don't understand. Why did you say it?'

Juliet shook her head. 'I don't know. Pique, I guess. Oh, Teresa, I've been here almost a fortnight, and I've made no progress with you whatsoever. You won't spend time with me, you won't let me help you, mostly you won't even speak to me. Even healthy hatred is better than indifference.'

Teresa was looking at her strangely. 'I really believe you care,' she exclaimed incredulously.

'Of course I care,' said Juliet, sighing. 'I didn't come here to play around on the beach. I came to help you to walk again, to become a real person again.'

Teresa compressed her lips, relaxing her fingers. 'Laura Weston only came because she wanted my uncle,' she said slowly. 'You see, Estelle told her all about him. That he was a Duque and wealthy and so on. I think she would have wanted him if he had been old and bald and ugly. As it was, she fell for him straight away.'

'Well, I can assure you, I didn't even know your uncle was a Duque until I arrived here. Unlike this Laura Weston, I should probably not have come if I'd known he was.'

Teresa seemed to be trying to understand. 'If – and I mean *if* – I let you help me, will you promise not to be in league with Estelle against me?'

'In league with Estelle!' echoed Juliet. 'Of course I'm not in league with Estelle. She isn't exactly my cup of tea.'

'What does that mean? You don't like her?'

'I wouldn't go so far as to say that!' amended Juliet hastily. 'It's just – well, she is a lot older than you and me, isn't she?'

And for the first time Juliet saw Teresa smile, properly, not the sneering grins she had been used to seeing. It brought a strange lump to her throat, and she sank down on the sand beside her, taking her hand.

'So – Teresa,' she murmured softly. 'Are we going to be friends?'

Teresa gave her a tremulous look. 'Oh, I – I suppose

so. Just don't try to stop me loving Felipe, that's all!'

Juliet did not answer this. This was a problem which would have to be solved at some future date.

In the days that followed Juliet grew to know the real Teresa, not the spoilt, unhappy individual she had been when confined solely with Nurse Madison for company.

Nurse Madison did not like her patient's sudden change of allegiance, but as Teresa had not confided its origin to her, she could do nothing. Instead, she spent her time following them around, except when they went out in the car, and she was not invited.

Juliet discovered that Teresa had quite a bright intelligence, and Teresa discovered that Juliet's sense of humour made their days bright and companionable. Francisco accompanied them often, stating quite cleary that he considered it was his influence which had broken the ice.

Sixteen days after his departure, the Duque returned.

Juliet did not know he was back until he joined them for breakfast, the morning after his arrival.

'Well, *pequena?*' he said to Teresa. 'How are you today?'

'Tio Felipe!' Teresa's face was alight with pleasure. 'When did you get back?'

'Late yesterday evening, *pequena*. And you, *senhorita*. Are you well?'

Juliet's colour deepened as usual. 'Thank you, *senhor*, I am fine.'

Teresa caught his hand, drawing him close to her side. 'Senhorita Summers and I are good friends now, Felipe. We have – how do you say it – ironed out our differences.'

The Duque seemed astounded. 'Is this so? Then I am very pleased. Senhorita Summers, I am very grateful to you.'

Juliet managed a slight smile, concentrating on the rolls on her plate. She wondered why he was so pleased – because of his affection for Teresa and his desire to see her well, or his desire to marry Estelle Vinceiro.

Teresa tugged at his hand, attracting his attention. 'I have also been in the water, Felipe. I cannot swim, but the Senhorita and Francisco, they help me!'

The Duque frowned. 'Francisco? Francisco Valmos?'

'That's right, *senhor*,' said Juliet, looking up. 'He is a friend of yours, is he not?'

'A friend of Estelle's perhaps,' remarked the Duque dourly. 'Tell me, *senhorita*, have you seen much of this young man?'

'We have spent much time with him,' interposed Teresa. 'He is an entertaining companion.'

The Duque snapped his fingers impatiently. 'Nevertheless, I would prefer it if in future you consult with me before making arrangements to go out with him, *senhorita*,' he said to Juliet, his eyes dark and enigmatic.

It was the first encounter Juliet had really had with him since the day on the beach at Lauganca Bay, and she felt the faint stirrings of torment which she was growing used to associating with him.

'Naturally as Señor Valmos was a guest in your house before you went away I assumed he was a friend of yours,' replied Juliet stiffly.

'It does not do to assume anything,' remarked the Duque bleakly. 'Well, Teresa, I am glad to see you looking so much better. It is to be hoped the improvement will continue.'

'I – I'm sure it will,' said Teresa, showing a trace of disappointment in her uncle's terse manner. 'Felipe, was the trip successful?'

The Duque had been staring across the patio broodingly, and seemed to find it difficult to draw his mind back to the present. 'What – oh – oh, yes, thank you, Teresa. Most successful.'

'That is good. And now that your business is over, perhaps you will be able to spend some time with us.'

The Duque shrugged his broad shoulders. Then he seemed to decide something, for he said: 'Tell me, Teresa, how well are you? Well enough to attend a small party this evening?'

Teresa's eyes darkened. 'Oh, I don't know, Felipe.'

Juliet finished her coffee, dabbed her mouth with her napkin and rose to her feet. If the Duque was about to begin making assignations with Teresa he could undo all the good Juliet had done.

'Will you excuse me, *senhor*,' she murmured politely, seeking the shade of the verandah.

'Wait!' The Duque's tone was peremptory, and she turned.

'Yes?'

'I should like you to attend this party also, Senhorita Summers.'

Juliet hesitated, and then said: 'No, thank you, *senhor*. I – well, I should feel out of place with your friends. Thank you for inviting me, but I must decline.'

Teresa was staring at him now, her eyes brighter. 'Then I shall go, Felipe,' she said. 'Yes, as Senhorita Summers says, it is time I began breaking out of the cocoon I have built around myself. Soon – soon I shall be able to walk, and I want to meet your friends before then.'

The Duque looked moody now, his eyes surveying Juliet with something like anger in their depths.

'Very well, Teresa,' he said tautly, looking at his niece now. 'You shall accompany me. It is a pity your companion is so staid, but I suppose it would not do for us all to be alike.'

Juliet listened to no more. She hurried indoors, aware of suppressing the strongest desire she had ever experienced. That of going out to a party with the arrogant Duque de Castro.

The following day, Teresa developed a severe cold. Long spells even in the warm waters of the Caribbean, had taken their toll, for once into the water, she never wanted to come out.

Juliet visited her, commiserated with her, and then left her to the doting ministrations of Nurse Madison.

She encountered the Duque in the main hall. Dressed as usual in riding gear, he had been out early, riding about the estate. When he was at home he invariably rode in the early mornings, so Teresa had told her. His lazy eyes surveyed the attractive picture she made in a short white pleated skirt, and a halter-necked blouse of red silk.

'So, *senhorita*,' he murmured, 'you have been visiting our patient.'

'Yes, *senhor*. I am afraid Teresa took too gladly to the roar of the waves.'

He inclined his head in silent agreement, and then said: 'And you, *senhorita*. What do you plan to do today?'

Juliet's legs felt a little weak. 'I – well, I suppose I will swim a little, or maybe play tennis with Miguel.'

'I see. In other words, you have nothing planned.'

'No, *senhor*.'

'No? That is good. I suggest we spend the day at Lauganca Bay. I will give you a few tentative lessons in skin-diving, *sim*?'

'*Senhor!*' She stared at him in surprise.

'Well? Does not the idea appeal to you?'

'Yes, but – well – I mean – Teresa!'

'Nurse Madison is only too willing to take care of your charge. And I must confess I do not feel like working today after such a long period of absence. So? Is this all right?'

Juliet compressed her lips. 'Very well, *senhor*.'

'Good. Get your swimming things and I will meet you on the forecourt in half an hour.'

'Yes, *senhor*.'

In her room, her fingers trembled as she stripped off her skirt and blouse and put on the black, one-piece swimsuit. Then she put on her clothes again, thrusting her bra and panties into the bag with her towel and beach coat. Sliding dark glasses on to her nose, she descended the stairs in time to meet Nurse Madison at the bottom.

'Are you going out, Miss Summers?' asked Nurse Madison curiously.

Juliet sighed. 'Just – just to the beach,' she replied casually.

'There's a letter for you,' said Nurse Madison. 'I was about to bring it up to you. Here you are!'

Juliet took the letter, recognizing Rosemary's hand-writing at once. 'Thanks,' she said awkwardly, expecting the nurse to turn and go, but she didn't, and Juliet thrust the letter into the bag, said *Cheerio* in a light tone, and walked out through the main doors on to the forecourt where a dark blue sports car was parked, with the Duque leaning against the bonnet, smoking a cheroot. Nurse Madison's eyes widened spitefully, and Juliet heaved a heavy sigh as she approached the car.

The Duque frowned. 'Is something wrong?'

'Nurse Madison will be hotfoot to tell Teresa that we are going out together,' she said exasperatedly.

The Duque grinned lazily, and opened the car door for her. 'Do you mind?'

Juliet gave him an old-fashioned look. 'Of course. Teresa is beginning to believe in me. I don't want her trust shattered.'

The Duque shrugged, as he climbed in beside her. 'Well, it is too late to worry now.' He switched on the ignition, put the car into gear, and they drove away fast. 'What do you think she will tell Teresa?'

'Oh, just the truth, I suppose. With certain additives.'

'Like what?'

'Like we might be . . .' Her voice trailed away.

'Like we might be what? Having an affair?' The Duque's tone was mocking.

'Something like that.'

'And that troubles you.'

Juliet gasped. 'You know perfectly well that Teresa is jealous of everyone who looks at you!'

He frowned. 'You exaggerate.'

'Not much, believe me. That's why she and Senhora Vinceiro could never be friends.'

'Why Senhora Vinceiro? Because she is my cousin? Because she is beautiful?'

'You are being deliberately obtuse,' said Juliet, forgetting for a moment to whom she was speaking.

The Duque raised his dark eyebrows. 'Indeed?'

'Yes, indeed. Oh, *senhor*, you know I'm right.'

'I know that I am growing tired of you calling me *senhor*,' he murmured, his eyes on her for a moment.

Juliet flushed. 'Would you have me call you Your Grace?'

'No.' His tone was taut now. 'I would have you call me Felipe.'

Her stomach plunged sickeningly, righted itself, and

then plunged again. She pressed a hand to her middle, and forbore to answer his remark.

Lauganca Bay looked even more beautiful than it had done before. Maybe that was because they were alone, she acceded to herself. The Duque was a stimulating companion, stimulating and disturbing!

They carried rugs, airbeds, and a hamper down to the beach, and Juliet busied herself arranging everything. The Duque had parked the car nearer the headland where the boathouse was situated, and it was only a stone's throw away from where they were picnicking.

'Tell me,' said Juliet, watching him with fascinated eyes as he unbuttoned his shirt, 'do not the conventions practised by your countrymen apply here?'

He frowned, pulling his shirt out of his pants lazily. 'In what way – er – what is your name?'

'Rosemary, but call me Juliet. I like it better.'

'So do I. Now – what conventions?'

'Well, I always understood that a Portuguese girl of good family would never spend time alone with a man unless they were married, or engaged, at least.'

He took off his shirt. '*Sim*, this is so.'

Juliet looked exasperated. 'Then what are we doing here?'

'You are not Portuguese, *senhorita*. You are English.'

'So that gives you the right to spend time alone with me?'

'You accepted my invitation – er – Juliet, did you not?'

Juliet hunched her shoulders, kicking the sand with her bare feet. 'I – I suppose so.' She moved restlessly. 'But I don't like the idea of being treated like – like a peasant!'

The Duque shook his head, and walked across to the boathouse, emerging a few moments later with a black rubber suit. He took off his trousers, revealing a pair of swimming trunks, much to Juliet's amused relief, and then proceeded to pull on the suit.

Within a few minutes he was ready, and said: 'Don't go away. I'll be right back,' and walked away into the water, disappearing after a few minutes into the depths.

Juliet sighed again, sat down on the sand, drew up her knees, and wrapping her arms round them, prepared to wait.

It seemed hours before he returned, and she was beginning to feel faint twinges of anxiety. Then he came up, out of the waves, like some black, shiny seamonster.

He pulled off his goggles and head covering as he approached her, smiling quite relaxedly.

'The water is turbulent,' he remarked, unzipping the body of the suit to his waist. 'But if we stay in the shallows, you should be all right. Can you get the other suit?' Juliet hesitated. 'What is wrong? Are you nervous?'

'No,' she denied fiercely, and walking into the boathouse, pulled off her skirt and blouse.

It wasn't as easy putting on the skin-tight suit as she had imagined. It clung to her hot skin, and she was sweating visibly when he appeared in the doorway.

'Go away!' she exclaimed irritatedly. 'I can manage.'

He merely smiled, and with a deft upward movement, brought the suit up her body, so that she just had to slide in her arms. She refused to thank him, feeling childishly annoyed that he had had to help her, and then emerged into the sunlight again, while he collected an oxygen cylinder.

It was not the most successful of lessons. Juliet was intent on not appearing too knowledgeable, and in consequence was doubly stupid. The Duque was marvellously patient, but at last she waded out of the water, pulling off the heavy cylinder which was almost weightless in the water.

'I'm tired,' she exclaimed, 'and hungry. Can we eat now?'

The Duque nodded amiably. 'If you like. Tell me, have you ever dived before?'

'Why do you ask that?' she prevaricated.

'Because I'd say you knew what you were doing, but didn't intend that I should know that. Did this – er – elderly woman you were companion to go skindiving, too? As well as driving through the Swiss Alps?'

Juliet found herself smiling at him, and then turned away before she was tempted to confide in him.

After lunch, a delicious meal of cold chicken and salad, with fruit and ice cream in small ice-cooled containers, followed by aromatic continental coffee, Juliet felt replete. After her dip in the sea, she had put on her clothes in the boathouse, not feeling relaxed enough to lounge around in a swimsuit with the Duque. Although today he seemed relaxed and informal, she could not forget his identity, and the touch of hauteur he seemed to maintain confirmed this belief.

Sitting, staring out to sea, watching the foaming breakers of the Atlantic splashing unceasingly over the rocks, she felt almost content. Her companion was lounging back on the sand, a cheroot between his teeth, studying the chart from the wall of the boathouse. Juliet smiled to herself. They could be any couple out for a picnic together, and it seemed incredible to realize that she was his niece's companion, and he was the aristocratic ruler of Venterra.

Only the thought of what Nurse Madison might have told Teresa disturbed her peace of mind. The older woman would use every weapon she could muster to get rid of Juliet, and this trip was a double-edged sword.

The Duque was watching her now, seeing the fleeting expressions crossing her revealing face. 'So, Juliet, what is wrong?' he murmured. 'You are bored, perhaps?'

Juliet shook her head vigorously. 'No, I'm not bored,' she denied swiftly.

'So? What is wrong?'

Juliet heaved a sigh. 'Oh, I was just thinking about Teresa.'

'Oh, yes?'

'Yes.' She looked at him for a moment, unwillingly

feeling the traitorous stir of her senses. But it was only a physical thing, she told herself fiercely, only a physical attraction!

'Juliet, tell me about yourself. Are your parents alive?'

'My father is. My mother died when I was born.'

'And he does not object to you crossing half the world to take a job in the West Indies?'

Juliet flushed. That was a difficult one. 'He – well, he doesn't have a great deal of time to think of anything,' she said honestly. 'He's a businessman, and he spends most of his time working.'

'You didn't answer my question,' the Duque remarked lazily, drawing on his cheroot. 'But no matter. How long do you expect to stay here?'

She lifted her shoulders. 'I – well, as long as I'm needed, I suppose, *senhor*.'

The Duque buried the stub of his cheroot in the sand impatiently. 'You deliberately refuse to use my name, do you not, Juliet?'

Juliet felt the heat sweep over her body at the husky note in his attractive voice. 'I – I do not think it is a good idea to use your Christian name, *senhor*. After all, I am only an employee!'

The Duque flicked a sand fly from his arm carelessly. 'Then, *senhorita*, as such, you should obey my commands.'

Juliet got jerkily to her feet. This had got to stop. These kind of conversations were provocative and dangerous, particularly as she was so vulnerable, and they were so isolated here.

'I – I think it is time we returned to the *quinta*, *senhor*.'

'Do you?' he got slowly to his feet, big and powerful, in whose hands she would be as helpless as a mouse with a tiger.

Juliet turned away from him, bending to lift a rug preparatory to folding it. As she straightened, she was aware of him close behind her, his breath fanning her neck, moving the tendrils of hair which had escaped from the braids bound round her head.

'I do not like this,' he said, pulling a strand of her hair so that she winced in pain.

'What, *senhor*?' she asked, still not turning.

'Your hair in this style. I prefer it loose. Loosen it!'

Juliet could hardly get her breath. 'Please, *senhor*,' she said chokily, 'let us go!'

She felt his fingers on the side of her neck, caressing her skin for a heart-stopping moment, and then he gave a harsh exclamation, and gathering up the picnic hamper and the airbeds, he strode away, up the incline towards the car.

Juliet could not move at once. Her legs felt like water and the palms of her hands were damp with perspiration. Oh God, she thought, sickly, I love him, *I love him!*

Closing her eyes for a moment in agony, she felt a wave of absolute misery sweep over her. She had thought she had troubles in England, she had thought she could escape from her father's possessiveness, only to find herself trapped in her own net. The Duque was an honourable man, Estelle Vinceiro was his future wife, there could be no deviating from his path, and the attraction he felt for her was the usual physical chemistry of a dark man for a fair woman.

She opened her eyes, saw him stowing the hamper in the car, and hastily gathered up the rest of the things and followed him. She slid into her seat silently, praying her composure would last until they reached the *quinta*.

The Duque got into the car, his thigh brushing hers, causing an electric current to run up her spine at the touch. Then he looked at her and said:

'I apologise, *senhorita*. Forgive me!'

Juliet shook her head, and said: 'It was nothing, *senhor*,' and then looked out of the side window of the car for the rest of the journey home. She was holding back the tears that trembled on the rims of her eyes with fierce concentration, and she knew then, for certain, that there is no escape from life.

CHAPTER SIX

WHEN they arrived back at the *quinta*, Juliet went straight to her room. Just now, she felt she couldn't face another human being, and the possibility that Teresa might question her in detail about the day's events terrified her. She didn't know how her precarious, newly-discovered emotions would stand up to such a strain.

In her room she stripped off her clothes, and going into the bathroom took a cooling shower. Then, wrapping herself in a bathrobe, she returned to the bedroom, lifting her basket-bag, and beginning to empty its contents. It was then that she came upon the letter.

All day it had lain there, but she had been so occupied with Felipe that its arrival had completely slipped her mind. With trembling fingers she slit open the envelope, and sinking down on to the side of the bed, she began to read.

Rosemary had begun the letter 'Dear Rosemary' as a cautionary measure, should the letter have fallen into the wrong hands. Although, as Juliet progressed through its three pages, she wondered why her friend had bothered. There were so many more implicating things in the letter that her name began to seem less than important.

It seemed that Robert Lindsay had indeed been absolutely furious when he received the letter that Rosemary had posted after Juliet's departure from London. He had, as they had both assumed, beaten a track straight to Rosemary's door, and demanded that, had she any knowledge at all of his daughter's whereabouts, she should give it.

'*I was positively a nervous wreck by the time he left,*' Rosemary continued. '*There was a great deal of talk about withholding information, and calling in the police and so on, but I think he was only bluffing, as your father is the last man in the world to welcome unnecessary publicity, and once you call in the police, it's practically impossible to prevent the press from finding out.*'

Juliet halted here, feeling an awful sense of anticlimax. Rosemary's letter brought back more vividly than any memories she could conjure up the whole miserable confinement of her life in England. How could any man in this year of nineteen hundred and seventy be so short-sighted? Couldn't her father see that her bid for freedom was a mental thing more than a physical thing? Didn't he understand his own daughter at all?

She reached for a cigarette, heaved a deep sigh, and then continued reading the letter.

'*Anyway, after a few days without any apparent signs of success, he contacted Daddy. Daddy naturally knew nothing of our arrangement, and I felt an absolute fraud lying to him. I don't think at the time we made our plans we really truly realized just how many people your father might involve.*'

'Then the most awful thing happened. My mother, who is as you know terribly softhearted, grew very sorry for your father, and decided to do a bit of detective work herself. She suggested that if you were going abroad it was logical to suppose that you wouldn't use your own passport because of being traceable, and so on....'

Juliet's mouth felt dry, and she could hardly stop her hand from trembling, making Rosemary's writing dance undecipherably before her eyes.

'Don't ask me why this idea sprang to her mind! Obviously your father had exhausted his inquiries in this country, and he seized on the idea. A swift examination of possible flight lists around the time of your disappearance revealed that a certain Rosemary Summers travelled on a B.O.A.C. flight to Barbados!'

Juliet flopped back on the bed. Oh, lord, she thought desperately.

'You can imagine how I felt! Particularly when tackled by a combined force of my parents and your father. But have no fear! I did not reveal your ultimate destination, and even though inquiries have been made in Bridgetown, your island retreat seems safe for the time being. Apparently, this man you're working for has his own private means of transportation, and as there are many many people in the islands with that same happy responsibility, your father has not found any evidence of your whereabouts so far.'

Juliet allowed herself a small sigh of relief at this news, but even so, she was well aware of her father's dogged determination, and when roused in this way, a way he had never before experienced, he would not give up lightly. She turned to the final page of the letter.

'So now I'm in the doghouse. My own parents have been a little more understanding. They realize that I can't break your confidence, but you know your father's methods of getting what he wants better than I do, and I think they're afraid he may use his influence against them in an effort to hurt me.'

Juliet sat up. This was intolerable. She could not allow Rosemary and her parents to be persecuted in this way. Of course she was well aware of her father's propensity for using any method available to gain his objective. Hadn't this been the reason for her escape in the first place? Heavens, whatever had made her think he might be less cruel this time? It was she who was being stupid and insensitive now. By involving Rosemary and her parents she was behaving in a careless and cowardly manner.

But what could she do? This taste of freedom, even with its accompanying heartache, was more important to her than anything had ever been. But sooner or later she would have to face her father, and if he was in any danger of attempting to persecute the Summers then she must act now and act swiftly.

She finished Rosemary's letter first. There were no recriminations from her, and Juliet thought how loyal and trustworthy a friend she really was. She knew of no one else who would have taken such a responsibility.

She paced the floor wearily, turning the problem

over in her mind again and again. There seemed little doubt that she would have to contact her father, and attempt, albeit perhaps uselessly, to make him realize her position, and to give her the credit for a little common sense.

A tap at her door heralded the arrival of Consuelo with a tray of tea. Juliet almost jumped out of her skin at the unexpected intrusion, still shakily aware of the tremulous state of her emotions. Momentarily those seconds with the Duque on the beach had been banished from her mind, but now they were back, their possible outcome thundering in her ears. Her own realization of her feelings for her employer seemed more terrifying than ever now when she was faced with the possible prospect of being forced to leave here immediately. Maybe she was insane; after all, most girls would have jumped at the chance to escape from such a state of futility, but Juliet could only imagine the emptiness of her life should she never set eyes on the Duque again.

Consuelo looked at her strangely, as she placed the tray of tea on the bedside table.

'The Senhorita Teresa is waiting to see you, *senhorita*,' she remarked, her usually cheerful features rather solemn. 'But the Senhor Duque said you would prefer to take your tea in your room.'

Juliet felt the hot colour surge into her cheeks. 'Oh, did he? Well, thank you, Consuelo.'

Consuelo nodded, gave a shrug of her ample shoulders, and departed. Juliet frowned, and then poured herself some tea, and sipped the hot, weak liquid gratefully. She despised herself for her own indecision. After all, why had she come here in the first place? Apart from her own selfish reasons of escape, of course. *To help Teresa!* And this was one item she was taking into little consideration. Was she so like her father that she could only think of herself and no one else? Unless her father was capable of buying and selling the Duque de Castro, which seemed highly unlikely, why need she feel afraid of him? He couldn't force her physically to return to England, *could he*? She was over twenty-one and her own mistress!

Even so, as she descended the staircase later, her fine words mocked her a little. When faced with Robert Lindsay would she collapse before his verbal barrage as she had done so many times before? Tonight she must decide the best method of approaching him.

But for the present there was Teresa, and the immediate prospect of explaining her day out with Felipe, which Nurse Madison had no doubt exaggerated out of all proportions.

In the hall, she encountered Miguel.

'Is the Senhorita Teresa still in bed, Miguel?' she asked, as casually as she could.

Miguel nodded. '*Sim, senhorita*. I understand the Senhorita is very poorly.'

'Very poorly!' echoed Juliet, frowning. 'But this morning she had a bad cold, that was all. In what way is she very poorly?'

Miguel shrugged his shoulders eloquently. 'Nurse Madison says she is very concerned about her condition,' he replied, and continued on his way out to the forecourt of the *quinta*.

Juliet bit her lip, heaved a sigh, and walked with forcedly determined steps towards Teresa's suite of rooms. It seemed inconceivable that within the space of half a day Teresa's condition which had seemed so slight this morning should have deteriorated to 'very poorly'.

Reaching Teresa's sitting room, which was deserted, she crossed it and knocked firmly on the door of her bedroom. The door was opened at once by Nurse Madison who came out, a finger pressed warningly to her lips.

Juliet felt rather impatient. 'What is the matter, Nurse Madison? Has something happened to Teresa? This morning she had a cold, nothing more, and yet now I hear that she is very poorly. Why?'

The older woman looked rather smug. 'As you must be aware, Miss Teresa is rather delicate, and while you might not find a cold a particularly trying occurrence, my patient is a slightly different matter.'

'Can I see Teresa, then?' asked Juliet, restraining any impulse she might have felt to vent some of the frustration she was feeling on Nurse Madison.

'She's sleeping at the moment,' replied Nurse Madison, with some satisfaction. 'I've advised her to stay in bed for the rest of the day at least. One should never take chances with invalids.'

Juliet twisted her hands behind her back. 'Teresa is hardly an invalid, Nurse Madison. The Duque has told me that her confinement to the wheelchair is not wholly a physical thing.'

'I suppose you mean that nonsense about psychological blockages, and so on,' exclaimed Nurse Madison scornfully.

'It's not nonsense,' returned Juliet, a little more sharply. 'Such paralyses do occur!'

'Indeed!' Nurse Madison stiffened her back. 'Well, I can only say that in my opinion, Miss Teresa will never walk again, without some form of support.'

Juliet compressed her lips. Her initial reaction was to have a verbal battle with this annoying creature whose methods of nursing were completely out of date, but a kind of inner instinct warned her that that was not the way. It was not inconceivable that Nurse Madison enjoyed her leisurely occupation here in such idyllic surroundings, and Teresa's improvement and possible subsequent recovery formed no part of her plans. Was it possible that she was deceitful enough to imagine she could get away with keeping Teresa an invalid as long as she wished her to be so? Obviously, Teresa's attitude and state of mind greatly assisted any plans of this kind, and her deliberate fostering of the girl's maliciousness towards anyone who genuinely tried to help her were not motivated by any real sense of vocation, with her patient's good health at heart, but rather by more personal desires.

Just then, Juliet heard Teresa call: 'Nurse, Nurse! Where are you?' in a rather plaintive voice.

Nurse Madison turned back to the bedroom door. 'I think you'd better go, Miss Summers. You must be the last person Miss Teresa wants to see.'

'Oh! Why?'

'Surely you don't need me to tell you that. I haven't spent the day with Miss Teresa's guardian!'

'What has that to do with it?'

Nurse Madison's expression was sneering. 'You know exactly what it has to do with it.'

'I know that you seem to encourage Teresa in some mistaken belief that her uncle has more than avuncular feelings towards her!' exclaimed Juliet, before she could prevent herself.

'How do you know what feelings the Duque has for her?' retorted the older woman angrily. 'The Duque has always taken an intense interest in his ward. Only a woman like Estelle Vinceiro could stir up the amount of trouble she has done — unnecessary spitefulness, I call it!'

'Nurse Madison, where are you?' Teresa's voice came again.

Juliet stayed the woman by taking her arm, preventing her from entering the bedroom. 'I think you have a little knowledge of spitefulness yourself, Nurse Madison,' she said coldly. 'How do you get your kicks? From taunting Teresa with every tiny piece of gossip you can hustle up?' She held on as Nurse Madison attempted to wrench her arm away. 'I don't think you care a jot for Teresa! There's only one person in whom you take the slightest bit of interest, and that is yourself!'

'How dare you! How dare you!' Nurse Madison was incensed.

Juliet released her arm. 'Go on, do your worst, but remember, the Duque is no fool, and even he will begin to have his suspicions if Teresa makes no progress!'

'You're talking absolute nonsense!' Nurse Madison was less convincing now, and then Teresa called again:

'Nurse Madison! What are you doing? Who are you talking to out there?'

'It's me, Teresa,' said Juliet, pushing past the older woman and entering Teresa's room.

She was astounded to discover that the shutters were closed, and no breeze penetrated their closeness. The room was slightly humid, and Teresa, in bed, covered with what seemed to be far too many blankets, was sweating profusely.

Realizing that on no account must Teresa get more of a chill, Juliet nevertheless removed some of the covers from the bed, and smoothed a towel from a nearby trolley over Teresa's flushed cheeks.

Teresa looked at her rather petulantly, and then said: 'You've been out with Felipe,' accusingly.

'That's right,' said Juliet, nodding, and sitting down on the side of the bed. 'We went to Lauganca Bay. He gave me a skin-diving lesson.'

'I see.'

Nurse Madison hovered angrily in the background, uncertain of her best means of approach.

'Did Nurse Madison tell you I had gone out with the Duque?' asked Juliet, taking Teresa's hand. It was hot too, and lay limply in her own.

'Yes.' Teresa twitched the coverlet with her other hand. 'My – my cold seems to have got worse.'

'I wonder why,' murmured Juliet dryly. 'Do you feel ill?'

'Not exactly. I feel awfully hot, and my throat's dry.'

'Then have a drink,' said Juliet, pouring a little iced lemon juice into a glass. 'Here,' she helped Teresa to take some, 'I really think you've not changed at all. Maybe Nurse Madison is unnecessarily concerned for your welfare.' This last was said with a little sarcasm that Nurse Madison could not fail to recognize.

Teresa struggled up on her pillows. 'Actually, I wanted to get up after lunch, but – well—'

'You're not fit to be up!' interposed Nurse Madison sharply.

'I would agree with you now,' said Juliet, looking round angrily at the nurse. 'She's obviously running a temperature, but whether that's due to the cold or to an overweight of blankets on a bed in a room which is absolutely stifling, I wouldn't care to hazard a guess!'

'Don't try to teach me my job!' said Nurse Madison furiously. 'The Duque shall hear about your interference!'

'I am hearing!' remarked a voice which Juliet could not fail to recognize, 'and quite frankly, I am inclined to agree with Miss Summers. You do appear to have hindered rather than helped Teresa's recovery.'

'Tio Felipe!' gasped Teresa, releasing herself from Juliet, and holding both hands out to her uncle eagerly. 'Oh, I've wanted to see you all day.'

Felipe took her hands, kissed them tenderly, and

then gently but firmly released himself. He looked at Juliet for a moment, and then said:

'Miss Summers, have you a complaint to make against Nurse Madison?'

Juliet moved awkwardly. She had no desire to get the woman dismissed, even if her methods left a lot to be desired. She felt sure that given time, she, Juliet, would be able to persuade Teresa to attempt those first steps at walking herself. To have the Duque dismiss Nurse Madison would be arrogant, and needlessly cruel. After all, she had no actual proof that her suspicions about the woman's motives were true.

'As I believe I said once before, *senhor*,' she said slowly, not looking at him, 'Nurse Madison's methods are perhaps a little out of date, that's all.'

'Very well.' The Duque bent his head in acknowledgement. 'We will give Nurse Madison the benefit of the doubt. Nevertheless, I do agree, it is hot and unhealthy in here. A little air – a little *Caribbean* air – never did anyone any harm.'

Nurse Madison flounced out, with barely a word, and Juliet made as though to do likewise. But the Duque motioned her to stay.

'So, *pequena*?' he murmured, looking at Teresa. 'You are happy now.'

Teresa looked at Juliet doubtfully. 'I suppose so, Felipe. Did – did you have a good day at the beach?'

The Duque shrugged his broad shoulders. 'I thought Miss Summers the rudiments of skin-diving,' he said, without actually replying to her question, Juliet noticed. 'Maybe one day you too will be able to skin-dive with us.'

Teresa sighed. 'Perhaps.'

The Duque moved towards the door. 'Tomorrow I must work, but the next day we will all take the hydroplane to Barbados, and do some shopping, eh?' He smiled. 'You would like that, *pequena*?'

Teresa's face lit up. 'Oh, yes, yes! Could we?'

'I do not see why not. After all, it is time you became used to mixing with the masses again. Who knows – we may find you something delicious to add to your wardrobe.'

After he had gone, Juliet's nerves relaxed. She had been tense in his presence, and yet after he had gone she felt an awful sense of despair. However, Teresa seemed completely recovered from any harboured thoughts of their day out together, so Juliet tried to feel content. But it was difficult when her whole body was aware of another being, so near, and yet so far from her.

After dinner that evening, Juliet found herself increasingly anxious about that letter. It was all very well shelving responsibility, when no one else was involved, but now her father had made everything far more complicated.

Then she had an idea. The Duque had said they might spend a day in Barbados in two days' time. If, *if* she could contact her father by some means, telling him she would be at his Club there at such and such a time, it might be possible to meet him; she had no doubt that Robert Lindsay himself would come if there was any chance of seeing her; and then she could personally explain why she had done what she had done, without actually giving her whole whereabouts away.

She lifted her shoulders helplessly. In theory that sounded perfectly all right. The trouble was her father had exercised such a powerful influence over her all her life, that even now she was in doubt of her own capabilities of standing up to him.

She paced about the room wearily, smoking cigarette after cigarette. It was the only way. The only sure way of absolving the Summers from all sense of responsibility, and the only way she could keep her own self-respect, and yet her knees quaked at the prospect. She half-smiled as she wondered how such a Victorian-inspired father could have sired such an independent anachronism. Did other girls, in other walks of life, have these kind of problems? She supposed some did, so why did she feel so completely isolated with her problem?

She wondered what the Duque might say if she confided the whole sorry story to him. He might be sympathetic, with his great understanding of people he might understand, but more likely he would consider her an irresponsible product of a society that bred such disobedience by its very essence, and that her father, as her guardian, had every right to dictate her life. At any rate she dared not take that risk, or with or without her father's intervention she might find herself back in London, imprisoned by the bars of financial success. Money might make the world go round, but for her it had developed into a racing carousel that was spinning her into oblivion.

Stubbing out her cigarette, she went downstairs to the lounge where the telephone had an extension. Lifting the receiver, she waited until the operator answered, and then asked for the number of the Hauser Reef Club, a luxurious hostelry where her father always stayed when he was in Barbados.

The manager answered, recognizing her when she identified herself in an undertone, hoping no one would overhear her conversation.

'Oh, yes, Miss Lindsay,' he said eagerly. 'I'm very glad to hear from you. Your father has been here for several days looking for you, but obviously without any success.'

'I know, Mr. Maxwell, I know,' said Juliet quickly. 'Look, do you know where he is now?'

'In London, I imagine, Miss Lindsay. It's several days since he departed for New York, en route for England.'

'I see. Well, look, Mr. Maxwell, I want you to do something for me.'

'Yes, of course, Miss Lindsay. What is it?'

'I want you to ring London, speak to my father or to my father's housekeeper, Miss Manders, and tell whoever it is you speak to that I'll be in Barbados, at the Club, on Friday at say – oh – three o'clock. Tell him if he wants to see me, to meet me there.'

'You'll be here, on Friday afternoon?' exclaimed the manager, with obvious astonishment.

'Yes, yes! Oh, Mr. Maxwell, don't waste any time. I know the time change and so on, and I know it will be the early hours of the morning in London, but if I know my father he'll still be awake. Do you know the number of his private house in Hampstead?'

'Of course, Miss Lindsay, I know the number. But are you sure you want me to ring him tonight?'

'You must, don't you see,' Juliet bit her lip nervously. 'He has got to have time to get here, and the sooner he knows that I'm alive and well, so to speak, the better!'

Mr. Maxwell accepted her explanation without further argument. Juliet was cynically aware that the information he had to offer Robert Lindsay would afford him a generous token of appreciation, and he had nothing to lose and everything to gain by contacting her father.

'Is that all right, then?' asked Juliet hastily, hearing sounds from the hall.

'Of course, Miss Lindsay. We look forward to seeing you.'

'Thanks,' said Juliet dryly, and rang off.

She walked jerkily to the hall door, looking out expectantly, ready with an explanation that she had been checking with the airport at Barbados about some discrepancy in her travelling expenses, but there was no one there. The hall was deserted.

Frowning, she made her way upstairs, reaching her room and closing the door thoughtfully. Then she promptly forgot about worrying whether anyone had heard her conversation when the whole prospect of what lay before her hit her with full force. She had got to think and think hard. There must be a way to appeal to her father, some way that would convince him that without this chance she would never be the same person he had always thought he knew.

The next day, true to his word, the Duque devoted all his time to the estate, riding out early in the morning and not returning until the evening. Despite her anxieties regarding her own personal problems, Juliet and Teresa resumed their companionable friendship, watched with malevolent eyes by Nurse Madison who seemed to have conceded that round to Juliet. Teresa seemed to have accepted her uncle's explanation that he had been giving Juliet a diving lesson, and that it had all been completely innocent.

Only Juliet wondered at its innocence. There had been that moment on the beach when both the Duque and herself had been aware of one another, but after all, there was nothing so unusual about that kind of a situation. She knew without any sense of false modesty that she was a passably attractive female, and the Duque's reactions had been those of any normal male placed in the same position. Her own reactions to him were an entirely different matter, but she did not fool herself that anything would come of it. Estelle Vinceiro was his race, his contemporary, and his type, and she would not be thwarted in her objective, of that Juliet was certain. And now that Teresa had taken to herself, Juliet, there seemed little doubt that Estelle would hasten the day when she became the mistress of the Quinta de Castro.

Late in the afternoon when Teresa was resting and Juliet was sitting on a lounger on the patio, reading, the Senhora Vinceiro herself was announced. She came towards Juliet, a wide smile on her small face.

'Oh, Rosemary,' she exclaimed, with enthusiasm, 'just the person I wanted to see!'

Juliet wondered why she felt so wary suddenly. Estelle had never been anything but friendly towards her, and yet she couldn't trust her and she didn't understand why. Obviously, now, with her new-found discovery of her own feelings, there was some constraint in her manner, but it was something more than that, and she despised herself for feeling that way.

'Hello, *senhora*,' she murmured awkwardly. 'Er – what did you want to see me about?'

Estelle seated herself opposite her on another lounger, and sighed. 'This really is the most heavenly place in the island,' she said, not at once answering Juliet's question. 'You must love it here already.'

'Oh, I do,' affirmed Juliet, nodding. 'But – but I think anywhere in these islands is delightful!'

'Do you? Do you now? Well, I suppose you may be right. It's just that when I think of the Caribbean I think of the Duque, and naturally Venterra is my special favourite as well as being my home.'

'Naturally,' murmured Juliet, feeling that some remark was warranted. 'Er – can I – can I offer you some tea?'

Estelle's smile was a little tight. 'In the *quinta* I feel completely at home,' she said. 'If I require tea I have only to ask for it.'

'Oh, oh, of course,' said Juliet awkwardly. 'I just thought. . . .' Her voice trailed away, and Estelle glanced around, apparently assuring herself that they were alone.

'Tell me,' she said, leaning forward, 'your – er – relationship to Teresa has improved intensively, I hear.'

'Teresa and I are good friends, if that is what you mean,' returned Juliet, a trifle dryly.

'Of course, of course. That is exactly what I meant. That is good. She has accepted you. Acceptance is *the* most important thing, don't you think?'

Juliet inclined her head, unwilling to make any comment.

'However, that is not entirely the whole of my reasons for speaking with you, Rosemary. I – er – I want to tell you something about Laura Weston.'

Juliet stiffened. 'Teresa has already told me a little about her previous companion, *senhora*,' she said politely.

Estelle's whole attitude, her casual use of her supposed Christian name, the almost confiding tone she was using, was intended to imply a confidence that Juliet was far from feeling.

'Yes, I suppose she has. After all, she was absolutely delighted when Laura made a positive fool of herself over the Duque. However, I think I can be a little more sympathetic about the whole affair.'

'I don't see what this has to do with me, *senhora*,' said Juliet, feeling slightly nauseated now.

'Don't you? Oh, well, perhaps not. Nevertheless, I feel I must tell you about Laura's unfortunate dilemma. You see—' Estelle glanced round yet again, '—you see, my dear, Laura was a rather – how shall I

135

put it? – er – attractive girl, and well – quite used to being pursued by men.' She gave a slight laugh. 'After all, Americans are noted for their pursuit of their women, aren't they? At any rate, when she came here, ripe for romance, as they say, and encountered the Duque, who even I must admit is quite devastatingly attractive, she misinterpreted the Duque's interest in her work as something much more personal.'

'How unfortunate!' murmured Juliet dryly.

'Yes, wasn't it?' Estelle put just the right amount of sympathy in her tone. 'And of course, when the Duque discovered her – well – penchant for him, he had no option but to dismiss her.' She sighed and gave an expressive gesture. 'Of course, in her case it was not a tragedy. She and Teresa had never gotten along. Their relationship had been stormy at the best of times, so that her departure was quite a relief, really.'

She rose to her feet, surveying her dainty sandals with a critical eye. 'But you, Rosemary, *you* are different. Teresa likes you, she has taken to you, and I really believe that with you she could make genuine progress, particularly as you appear to have that odious Madison woman taped from the start. I never liked her, of course, and the sooner she can be dismissed the better.'

'Thank you for your confidence in me,' said Juliet, biting her lip. 'Is – is that all, because if so—'

'No. No, Rosemary, not quite all.' Estelle compressed her lips, obviously looking for words to phrase her next statement. 'The fact is, I came here yesterday when you were out with the Duque. Consuelo told me.'

Juliet had known this was coming all along. And now it was here, and she felt frozen.

'Oh, yes,' she managed, in a tight little voice.

'Yes.' Estelle compressed her lips again. 'My dear Rosemary, I have no desire to offend you, but – well, I am afraid you might fall into the same trap as did poor Laura.'

'I don't think—' Juliet began, only to be interrupted.

'Wait, please. I know you are a sensible girl, and I don't want you to misunderstand me, Rosemary, but as I have said, the Duque is the kind of man whom women seem to find irresistible—'

Now Juliet interrupted Estelle. '*Senhora!* I can set your mind at rest. I am perfectly aware of your position, and of that of the Duque. And I am also not foolish enough to imagine the passing interest the Duque showed in me yesterday, by taking me to Lauganca Bay, when he was probably bored, as anything more than what it was.'

Estelle stopped moving about restlessly, and stared at her. 'I really believe you mean that, Rosemary.'

'Of course I mean it,' exclaimed Juliet, a little angrily, angry because inside her heart felt as though it was being torn apart by the strength of her emotions. But it was not love. That moment of revelation on the beach was not love. It could not be. It was infatuation. Love was a gentle thing, not this ravening monster that held her in its thrall.

Estelle smiled, rather smugly, Juliet thought. 'I'm so glad you understand, my dear. It's very difficult for me to have to broach such a subject, but Felipe seems to have no idea of the effect he has on susceptible females.'

'I am not a susceptible female,' said Juliet tightly. 'Unlike Portuguese women, British women are encouraged in gaining complete independence, and the Duque is by no means the most attractive man I have met!' She said this with vehemence, causing Estelle's eyes to narrow slightly.

'You mean you have known a lot of other men?' questioned the older woman, her eyes enigmatic.

Juliet shrugged her shoulders. 'Of course,' she said, forcing a light tone. 'You don't imagine British women marry the first man who takes an interest in them, do you?'

Estelle shrugged. 'Of course, your ways are not our ways. I forget.' This was said with just that touch of arrogance, making Juliet feel wholly inferior.

'Is that all, then, *senhora*?' Juliet rose to go. She wanted to get as far away from Estelle as the *quinta* would allow. Her earlier suspicions of Estelle Vinceiro had been realized. She could be just as ruthless as anyone could be when there was a chance of her plans being thwarted. Juliet began to wonder whether Laura Weston's abrupt dismissal had been wholly justified. Maybe she had become interested in the Duque, and Estelle, afraid of competition, had exaggerated the girl's feelings into something distasteful to a man as fastidious as the Duque de Castro.

And on the heels of this thought came another. That first day when in her anger she had told the Duque that Teresa was in love with him had resulted in an immediate response. If Estelle was insinuating her opinions into his mind at every turn he might find it difficult to distinguish what was truth and what was not. Obviously Estelle was obsessed with the idea that every woman who laid eyes on the Duque might have designs on him, and he had probably ignored her remarks to begin with. But when she, Juliet, had accused Teresa, she had unwittingly put more power into Estelle's hands by supporting her. Heavens, she thought, what a situation! She was tempted to put the whole affair behind her and return to England with her father if he indeed was there to meet her tomorrow.

But she knew she would not – she could not! This was something she had to see through to the end, even if that end was anathema to her. And there was always Teresa, who in time, Juliet was sure, would realize the futility of her feelings for a man old enough to be her father.

And Teresa needed Juliet, that was certain, now that Estelle had revealed herself in her true colours. Estelle didn't care about anybody but herself. Teresa was just an unnecessary encumbrance, for whom she had to find a companion, to free the Duque for more personal motives. If, through changing companions, Teresa suffered, that was just part of the pattern.

Estelle now was all smiles. 'It's so good to know I have an ally in you, Rosemary,' she said silkily, but Juliet just shook her head, and somehow walked blindly towards the entrance to the *quinta*. She dare not speak. For once her emotions ruled her head, and she couldn't have cared less what construction Estelle placed on her abrupt departure.

CHAPTER SEVEN

THE next morning dawned bright and clear, a wonderful morning, and yet Juliet found it difficult to drag herself out of bed. Apart from the mental torture of spending a day in the Duque's company, she had the daunting prospect of her father to face and some sort of excuse to offer to the Duque as to why she should want some free time alone in Bridgetown. Of course, as she had not officially had any free time since arriving on Venterra he could hardly object, but he would be bound to be curious.

When, dressed in a slim-fitting sheath of scarlet linen, with a scooped-out neckline and no sleeves, she went down to the patio for breakfast, she found the Duque himself breakfasting with Teresa, the sound of the girl's laughter echoing warmly round the impressive environs of the courtyard of the *quinta*.

He rose at her approach, wished her *Bom dia,* and waited until she was seated at the glass-topped table before reseating himself. His expression was enigmatic, and she wished she knew what he was thinking. The previous evening he had dined out, and although she knew she was stupid, the memory of that explosive moment on the beach continued to haunt her thoughts.

'Are you ready for our trip?' he asked politely, and Juliet nodded.

'Yes, *senhor*. But – well, there was something I wanted to ask you about that.'

'Oh, yes?' His tone was guarded.

'Yes. Er – would it be all right if I took a couple of hours off, while we are in Bridgetown?'

'A couple of hours off?' He frowned. 'Forgive me, what am I supposed to gather from that remark? Surely this day in Bridgetown's hardly working.'

Juliet flushed. He was making it extremely difficult for her.

'I know it sounds ungrateful, *senhor,* but since my arrival here over three weeks ago, I have not had any actual free time. By this–' she hastened on, '—by this I mean time away from either my employers or my employer's establishment.'

The Duque's expression was glacial. 'I see. I am afraid I have overlooked this point. Perhaps I was foolish enough to imagine that the simple tasks allotted to you here did not actually constitute work. It seems I was mistaken. Of course, Miss Summers, you may take *a couple of hours off!*'

Juliet shrank within herself. Even Teresa was looking hurt and distressed, and she felt an absolute heel. But how could she explain her real reasons?

Such an inauspicious beginning to the day did not augur well for the trip. The hydroplane transported them smoothly across the expanse of sea and islands towards their destination, but conversation was stilted, and Juliet half-wished she had waited until later to ask for those few hours of freedom. Now she had blighted not only her own, but Teresa's, day. As for the Duque, he seemed silent and remote, without even his usual gentle tenderness towards his ward.

In Bridgetown they lunched at a hotel in the city centre, where they could watch the sometimes amusing antics of the policemen on their points, and the kaleidoscopic panorama of humanity that passed beneath their windows. Teresa was enchanted with the donkeys in the high streets, anxious to visit the market and the waterfront, so that when the hands on the clock crept round to two-thirty Juliet did not think it would be too difficult to effect her escape. The Duque had a car on the island, and it had been awaiting them at the airport, and Juliet vaguely imagined that he would take Teresa on a sightseeing tour after lunch, leaving her free to keep her assignation.

However, when she suggested that now would be a suitable time to leave, the Duque failed to respond in the manner she had expected.

'Tell me, *senhorita*,' he murmured, as they stood beside the luxurious automobile, parked irreverently in a *No Parking* area, Teresa sitting patiently in the front sea, 'am I wrong, or do you have some assignation to keep?'

The hot colour surged into her cheeks, and she moved uncomfortably beneath those piercing dark eyes.

'Please, *senhor*,' she exclaimed, 'can you not allow me these few minutes of free time without requiring a detailed explanation of everything I do?'

The Duque's expression darkened. 'No, I cannot, *senhorita*!' he replied, his tone suppressing the anger she could feel that was emanating from him. 'While you are in my employ I will know where and how and with whom you spend your time!'

Her emotions drawn to a taut, feverish thread, Juliet felt an unreasoning fury at his arrogant words.

'Just who do you think you are talking to?' she exclaimed angrily. 'I may be in your employ, but you don't *own* me!'

'*Senhorita,* you overstep yourself,' he snapped furiously.

'It is you who overstep yourself, *senhor*!' she retorted, uncaring of the interested, speculating glances that were being cast in their direction.

'*Senhorita,* I am known in Barbados, and I do not intend that you should make a fool of me, and incidentally yourself, in the heart of its capital,' he muttered violently, and almost without her realizing what he was doing, he opened the rear door of the vehicle, thrust her inside, and slammed the door after her; climbing into the front, and setting the car in motion before she had time to gather her startled wits.

'How dare you!' she gasped, leaning forward, and even Teresa seemed astounded at her guardian's uncharacteristic behaviour. She looked at him sideways, and said:

'Surely Senhorita Summers is entitled to do as she pleases, Tio Felipe!'

The Duque gave her a stony glance. 'This is nothing to do with you, Teresa, and you will please to keep out of it.' He swung the car recklessly round a corner, causing Juliet to cling on to her seat, and then said: 'If you will tell me your destination, *senhorita,* I will take you there.'

Juliet compressed her lips. The Hauser Reef Club was hardly the type of place a girl of limited means would choose as a meeting place. Then, her anger overriding other considerations, she made up her mind. After all, the Duque would not know why she was going there; it would do him good to have something he couldn't understand to think about.

Biting her lip, she leant forward again. 'The Hauser Reef Club,' she said coldly. 'You'd better hurry. I have to be there for three o'clock!'

'Do not give me orders, *senhorita,* or you may find yourself in even greater difficulties than you are at present!' he snapped, and Juliet felt suitably chastened. Despite her brittle words, she hated this, and she wished she could just have met her father without all this hateful antagonism.

The Hauser Reef Club was outside Bridgetown, on the coast, luxurious, opulent, standing in brilliantly colourful surroundings, its kidney-shaped swimming pool overhung by frangipani, jessamine and scarlet hibiscus.

Guests were accommodated in individual chalets in the grounds, each with its own special charm of surroundings, all within sight and sound of the sea. A large clubhouse accommodated the restaurant and nightclub, but meals could be served in guests' chalets if required.

As the Duque swung round the central forecourt, to halt before the colonnaded entrance to the clubhouse, and Juliet slid swiftly out of the car, a tall, broad, middle-aged man came eagerly out of the swing doors, hastening down the steps to greet her. His dark hair, tinged with grey, his expression anxious, and maybe a few more lines to his forehead, were all so suddenly dearly familiar to Juliet, that words were unnecessary, and at his relieved cry of 'Juliet!' she ran across and was gathered closely into his arms. Only the harshly slammed door of the Duque's car, and his swift, wheel-churning departure, marred the moment for Juliet.

But then her father commandeered her thoughts, to the exclusion, for a while, of all else.

'My God!' he muttered, when at last he released her, only to place an arm about her shoulders. 'If you ever do that to me again. . . . .' He shook his head. 'What in hell do you think you're doing? When I got Maxwell's message I was practically at my wits' end!'

Juliet composed herself, and they walked across the exotically green lawns to Robert Lindsay's chalet. Once there, they seated themselves on the verandah, overlooking the creaming waters of the blue Caribbean, and a steward brought *daiquiris*. Juliet lit a cigarette, and relaxed a little, putting all thoughts but those concerning her father out of her mind.

'Now,' said Robert Lindsay, after he had lit himself a cigar, seating himself closely beside her, as though afraid she might suddenly disappear again in a puff of smoke. 'What's going on?'

Juliet ran a finger along a pleat in her skirt. 'Well, Daddy, you know perfectly well what's going on. I got myself a job.'

146

Robert Lindsay studied his daughter's bent head. 'Why?'

'Do we have to go into all that again? I've told you time and again, I want some independence. All my life you've made every decision there was to be made about my life. You've chosen my schools, my friends; you were even in the process of choosing my husband! Good lord, can't you see how terrible for me that is?'

Her father frowned. 'Juliet,' he said heavily, 'in this world, there are only two kinds of people: the winners and the losers! I'm – well, I won't say lucky enough, because I don't consider what I have achieved I have achieved by luck, but I will say I'm in that lucky bracket of being one of the winners!'

'Oh, Dad!'

'What's wrong now?'

'This is the same argument you always make! Heavens, life's not as simple as that! Some of the winners, or people you would call winners anyway, aren't winners at all, they're losers! And vice versa. You judge everything on a purely monetary basis! That's why you won't let me choose my own friends. You think that if people are financially inferior, they're socially inferior. It just isn't true!'

'Well, go on. We'll agree to differ on that point,' said Robert Lindsay, chewing his cigar. 'We're drifting from the point anyway. Why did you go to such lengths to hide what you were doing?'

'Oh, come on!' Juliet stared at him incredulously. 'You know why I hid what I was doing! Because if I'd told you – or rather, asked you – you would have ridiculed the whole business.'

'So instead you chose to ridicule me!'

Juliet compressed her lips, lifting her shoulders helplessly. 'Oh, Dad, it wasn't like that! I only wanted to be able to do what I wanted for a change. I wanted a job, to be able to say I *earned* that money, it wasn't just given to me, by *you*! How would you like to have to ask for everything you wanted, and only have it granted if the person you were asking thought it was the right thing for you!'

'I am your father!' he muttered gruffly.

'I know that! But I'm twenty-one, Dad. Not some sixteen-year-old, without any sense of values. I have a sense of values. I know what is worthwhile in this world, and what is not! I know that I've achieved something as a person – as a human being, if you like – by doing what I've done.'

Robert Lindsay rose to his feet, and paced about the verandah floor, sometimes studying her, and sometimes studying the floor at his feet.

'You realize what a shock this has been to Mandy, of course.'

Juliet sighed. 'Of course. Oh, Daddy, stop trying to make me feel a heel. Do you think I don't feel one already?' Then she looked up at him squarely. 'But I must tell you, I didn't get in touch with you because I wanted to. I got in touch with you because of the way you're catechizing Rosemary and her parents!'

'The Summers?' Robert Lindsay snorted angrily. 'That girl – that Rosemary – she knew where you were all right.'

'Yes, she did. But she would never have told you. That's the sort of person she is! She has integrity! A quality neither one of us possess in any great measure!'

'You're talking drivel!' exclaimed her father impatiently. 'Where does integrity get you in this world? I'll tell you – nowhere!'

'In your world, maybe,' said Juliet quietly. 'But in the world I'm discovering for myself, it exists all right. There are actually people who don't use dollar or pound or franc or deutschmark in every sentence they compose. Who don't care whether this or that company has gained or lost on the stock market; who don't *use* people!'

Robert Lindsay stopped his pacing. 'I never knew you hated me so much,' he said heavily.

Juliet clasped her hands. 'I don't hate you!' she exclaimed vehemently. 'Daddy, I love you. And for all that I've been terrified that you would find me before I was ready to let you find me, I've missed you! Not all the time perhaps, not always consciously, but when I saw you today, now, standing on the steps of the clubhouse, I didn't know how I'd had the courage to make the break!'

Her father's expression lightened, and he went down on his haunches before her, taking both of her hands in his. 'Juliet, Juliet,' he muttered huskily, 'do you know why I do what I do? Do you know why I fight every rival that comes my way, why I attempt to destroy every company that threatens our livelihood? I do it all for *you*. Yes, you, baby! My baby! The only living memory I have of the dearest and gentlest wife a man could ever have!'

Juliet felt the hot tears pricking at her eyes. Even while he was protesting his love, and that love was real, she knew that, she was afraid; afraid that this was all some devious, calculated method of gaining her confidence yet again. They had had rows before, plenty of rows, and always her father knew instinctively the best and most successful way to win his own way.

With an immense effort, she contained her tears, and said:

'I'm not going back, Daddy. Not yet, anyway.'

Robert Lindsay rose immediately to his feet, releasing her hands, and lifting his drink swallowed half of it at a gulp.

'Do you think I'll let you stay?' he said quietly, but ominously.

Juliet shrugged her shoulders. 'You can't stop me.'

'So you fondly imagine.'

Juliet pressed the palms of her hands against her hot cheeks. This was what she had feared. The usual pattern, explanations, recriminations, pleading, and finally – attack!

She smoked her cigarette. She would not allow him to hear the tremble in her voice. She would not give him the chance to undermine what small defences she might have. The only way to defeat such implacability was by being calm, and cool, and composed.

Gathering her composure about her, she said calmly: 'How is Mandy, anyway?'

Her father shrugged his broad shoulders. 'She's well,' he said shortly.

Juliet felt a moment's half-hysterical amusement. She had expected him to express Miss Manders as being grief-stricken at the very least.

She continued to smoke her cigarette, and at last he turned. 'Damn you, Juliet, you won't make a fool out of me!'

Juliet bent her head, and did not reply.

'Where are you working? Who is employing you? What are you doing?' The questions came sharp and fast.

Again Juliet did not reply.

Her father became really angry then. 'Do you imagine that by seeing me you'll have assuaged any anger I might feel against your friends the Summers?' he muttered furiously.

Juliet looked up. 'What do you mean by that?'

'I mean that if you thwart me, if you escape to this island retreat of yours, wherever it might be, and I have to return to London alone, you'll have made things worse and not better for them!'

Juliet's hurt resentment almost choked her. So much for the lovable, more sinned against than sinning parent of a few minutes ago. How could he? How could he?

She drank some of her *daiquiri*, aware of his eyes upon her, and then looked up at him with eyes swimming with unshed tears.

'If you attempt to interrogate the Summers, or make their lives impossible by some devious method you might find, then the whole sorry story will be told to the papers, and you know what a beanfeast they'll make out of it!'

'As you're so fond of telling me, the Summers have integrity,' retorted her father sarcastically. 'They wouldn't do such a dastardly thing!'

Juliet got unsteadily to her feet. 'No, perhaps not. But I would!'

Her father stared at her in amazement, and then an unwilling light of admiration lit his harsh features.

'Damn you, Juliet, I believe you would!' he muttered in astonishment.

'Make no mistake about it!' said Juliet unevenly. 'I'm *your* daughter, remember?'

Robert Lindsay stubbed out his cigar, and lit another.

'And you're not going to tell me where you're staying?'

'No.'

'Why? What if I agree to let you stay if you tell me?'

Juliet wiped her eyes with the back of her hand. 'Integrity is a dirty word to you,' she said. 'Do you think I could trust you?'

'You might try.'

'No, thanks.' She lifted her handbag. 'Are you going to let me go?'

'Do I have any choice?'

'Not really. I meant what I said.'

'I know you did.' He sighed heavily. 'When will you come home?'

Juliet bent her head, shaking it. 'I don't know. Maybe soon — maybe not. Have I still got a home to come back to?'

'In spite of everything, you mean? Of course. You're my daughter, Juliet, and a damn fine one, I suppose, only I'm too bloody pig-headed to see it. All right, I admit it. I want to run your life. I want to approve of the man you'll eventually marry. Is that so bad?'

'In moderation, no. But nothing with you is in moderation. You do everything on the grand scale.'

'So I can tell all your friends back in London that they need have no aspirations in your direction?'

'If you mean boy-friends, yes, you can safely tell them that.'

Her father shook his head. 'What is it you're searching for, Juliet?'

She shrugged her slim shoulders. 'I don't really know.'

He gave a heavy sigh. 'I only hope you do know what you're doing. I'd hate to see you get into a situation that you couldn't handle. There are plenty of men in the world, just waiting for the opportunity to meet someone like you.'

'I'm not naïve, Dad. I do know about the birds and the bees, you know.'

'Maybe, maybe. All right, Juliet, go your own way. But remember, I'll always be there, if ever you need me.'

In the taxi going back to Bridgetown, Juliet kept

glancing back, out of the rear window, assuring herself she was not being followed, but the road at that hour of the afternoon was deserted.

Relaxing in her seat, she found other problems crowding her mind. Most prominent of all, that of the Duque de Castro. During lunch, she had tentatively suggested that she met them back at the hotel for afternoon tea at five o'clock, but after the Duque's incensed departure, she was not certain he would be there. However, after paying the taxi-driver, a glance in the hotel car-park confirmed that the Duque was in the building, and she walked through the wide entrance hall looking about her with some trepidation.

Eventually, a word to the receptionist informed her that the Duque and his niece were having tea in the hotel lounge, and she entered the high-ceilinged room on rather unsteady legs, making her way towards them very nervously. Despite her calm departure from her father, she still felt strung up, and unready for any more verbal battles with anyone.

Teresa smiled at her arrival, and said: 'You're late, *senhorita*. It's already five-fifteen!'

Juliet managed a smile in return, trying to ignore the Duque's forbidding countenance. 'Am I? I'm sorry. The traffic. . . .' She allowed the sentence to trail away into nothingness.

The Duque, who had risen at her arrival, indicated that she should sit down, and gladly she did so, while he summoned the waiter for more tea.

'No – really—' began Juliet, only to be silenced by the cold glance he cast in her direction.

154

Teresa for her part seemed completely aware of the antagonism between her guardian and her companion, and Juliet wondered what construction she would place upon it.

When the tea came, she poured herself a cup, offering Teresa and the Duque in turn the same. Teresa accepted a second cup, but the Duque merely looked bored, shaking his head, as though he would have preferred something rather stronger.

Teresa, unable to suppress her curiosity, said: 'The Hauser Reef Club seemed a wonderful place!' enthusiastically.

Juliet smiled a little wryly. 'Yes – yes, it is.'

'Have you finished your – er – business, now, *senhorita*?' said the Duque suddenly, startling Juliet so that she spilt some of her tea on the immaculate table cloth.

Swallowing hard, she nodded. 'Yes – thank you.'

'Good.' He rose to his feet abruptly. 'I will be in the car park when you have finished. Will you wheel Teresa's chair outside?'

Teresa looked surprised now. 'Can't I come with you, Tio Felipe?'

The Duque shook his head. 'Keep Senhorita Summers company. I do not expect she will take long.'

In truth, Juliet felt that food would choke her, but rather than appear like a scared rabbit, she drank two cups of tea, smoked a cigarette, and made polite conversation with Teresa before agreeing to leave.

Driving to the airport, Juliet expected more questions from Teresa about her assignation, but to her surprise, apart from that one reference to the Club, Teresa said nothing more.

In the hydroplane, the Duque sat with the pilot, and it was getting late by the time they landed on the waters of Venterra Bay, Miguel was waiting with the car, but the Duque drove, with Miguel beside him, and Juliet and Teresa in the back of the car, to the *quinta*.

After such an exhausting day, Juliet was not surprised when the Duque advised Teresa to dine in her room as he was going out. Juliet wondered where he was going, and assumed Estelle Vinceiro had some part in his plans. She herself was glad to gain the sanctuary of her bedroom, and when Consuelo brought her dinner on a tray, she merely picked at the lobster and fruit.

It was very late when she heard the sound of the Duque's car returning to the *quinta*, but her nerves tensed in spite of everything that had happened.

Her interview with her father had receded into the background again, assuming the proportions of a dream now that she was back here on Venterra. At least now she didn't have to worry about Rosemary and her parents, and her father seemed to have accepted that her will was as strong as his.

CHAPTER EIGHT

Two days passed during which time Juliet saw very little of the Duque. He seemed continually out and about his estate, talking with the estate managers, dining out with friends, and generally living a life apart from the *quinta*. Once Estelle visited, but she again came while Teresa was resting in the afternoon, and Juliet was forced to listen to the detailed plans the Senhora had to put into operation once she was married to the Duque.

Teresa spent less and less time with Nurse Madison, seeming to realize that actual movement, normal movement that is, proved more satisfying than mere exercises. In the water she was becoming quite proficient, and with the aid of a rubber ring could propel herself quite energetically. Juliet felt convinced that it was only a matter of time before she asked for sticks or crutches in an effort to put life into limbs long unused. Whether Teresa's condition was the result of actual spinal damage that no one could find, or merely the psychological blockage, the specialists seemed to think was immaterial. She had not used her legs for so long she had forgotten how to walk, how to balance herself. But once she made those first initial efforts, Juliet felt sure her progress would make leaps and bounds.

Francisco Valmos visited them one morning, and in

his company Teresa blossomed becomingly. Juliet, aware of Francisco's admiration of herself, encouraged him to spend time with Teresa alone, hoping his company would in some way assuage the bitterness of the Duque's marriage to Estelle when it actually happened.

In truth, of all of them, Francisco seemed to possess the knack of persuading Teresa to have more confidence in herself. He complimented her on the healthy tan her legs were acquiring from hours spent on the beach, and admired her dress and the pretty, loose way Juliet had dressed her hair.

They were all having morning chocolate together when the Duque arrived back at the *quinta* unexpectedly early. His expression was dour when he saw Francisco, although he was forced to greet the young man politely, and make a casual remark. But his eyes were inscrutable, and Juliet was astonished when he said to her:

'*Senhorita!* I should like to speak with you in my study, if you have the time, of course!' This last was said with some sarcasm.

Juliet glanced questioningly at Teresa, who shrugged, and then getting to her feet said: 'Of course, *senhor*.'

She followed the Duque into the *quinta*, and across the hall to the study she had not entered since the first day of her arrival. The Duque waited until she was inside, and then closed the door firmly, and walked briskly across to his desk. Dressed in riding clothes, a dark green silk shirt open at the throat, he looked darkly attractive, the forbidding expression he wore adding to his almost animal magnetism.

'Sit down,' he said coldly, and she complied, mainly because her legs felt weak and unable to support her.

'Is something wrong, *senhor*?' she asked uneasily, aware of the tension in the room, like a living, tangible thing.

The Duque stood behind his desk, taking a cheroot from the box on his desk almost absently, and lighting it while his eyes appraised her inscrutably. Then he said:

'Tell me, *senhorita,* why did you come here?'

Juliet was startled. Whatever did he mean by that? Had he somehow discovered her real identity?

'I – I don't understand, *senhor*,' she said unevenly. 'You know why I came here. To help Teresa.'

'Indeed!' His tone was biting, and caught Juliet on the raw.

'Can you deny that I have helped her?' she exclaimed indignantly.

He shrugged, and did not reply. Then he said: 'You realize, of course, that your probationary period of one month is nearing its close.'

Juliet bent her head. 'Yes, I had realized that, *senhor*.'

He frowned. 'I confess, *senhorita,* your behaviour causes me some misgivings. Despite your undeniable friendship with my niece I have the feeling that her disablement was not the whole of the reason that brought you to Venterra.'

Juliet flushed. 'What are you trying to say, *senhor*?'

The Duque brought his fist down hard on the table, causing Juliet to jump nervously. 'All right, *senhorita*. You are the one who has always professed to like plain speaking, I will give you some. I believe you came to Venterra because you knew at some time you would be able to go to Barbados to meet your – your – *man-friend!*'

Juliet could almost have laughed, hysterically, at the Duque's words, had not the situation been so precarious.

'He is not my – my man-friend, *senhor*,' she said, with more composure than she was feeling.

The Duque's expression was disbelieving. 'Come now,' he said. 'You really don't expect me to believe that!'

Juliet felt angry suddenly. Even if she had met a friend in Barbados, what business was it of the Duque's? How dared he catechize her like this?

'What I do in my own time is my business, *senhor*!' she said angrily. 'If this is the way you treat your employees then I am not surprised you find it difficult to find them!'

'What do you mean?' He was dangerously quiet in his speech now.

'I mean Laura Weston – I've been told in some detail how Miss Weston became infatuated with you and was dismissed because of it! Maybe this is just some trumped-up story to cover your own inadequacies!' Even as she said the words, Juliet knew they were not true. He was just not that kind of man, but somehow she had to assuage the bitterness she was feeling, and just then she didn't particularly care who she hurt.

The Duque came round the desk in three strides, reaching her side in seconds, hauling her up out of her seat savagely, thrusting his face close against hers, terrifying her.

'That man you met so emotionally in Barbados was Robert Lindsay!' he muttered violently. 'A millionaire, no less, no doubt with commitments in England which prevented you from meeting openly! Not to mention the publicity if you were caught, of course! A man more than twenty years your senior, a man of ruthlessness in business, a man without any apparent conscience! Do you know he has a daughter older than you are?'

Did she know it? Now Juliet really felt hysterical. She struggled impotently to free herself, but the Duque's slender hands were surprisingly hard and strong, and they bit into the soft flesh of her upper arms with deliberate cruelty.

'How – how do you know who – who he was?' she asked, a little faintly.

The Duque's dark eyes were burning with the strength of his anger. 'I'll tell you how I know! Because after you and your – your—' he bit off an angry epithet, 'after you had disappeared into Lindsay's chalet, I returned to the Hauser Reef Club and made certain inquiries!'

'Oh, no!' Juliet felt despairing. 'Did – did the steward at the Club know you?' she asked bitterly.

'Maybe, maybe not. Why? Are you afraid he might

find out where you are staying? Of course,' he gave a brief mirthless laugh, 'maybe you ran away from him! Why didn't I think of that? Maybe you fancied a change, and Lindsay wouldn't agree to it!' He gnawed at his lower lip, unaware that Juliet was almost giddy with the pain in her arms. 'And now that the grand reconciliation has taken place, are you afraid he will find you are with me and be jealous? After all, what further heights await you after unlimited wealth? Only perhaps a *title*!'

'I – I think you're – you're mad!' she groaned, and the Duque became conscious of his cruelty.

With a stifled exclamation, he released her and she swayed faintly, hardly aware of anything but the agonizing pain of blood surging back where numbness had been before. The Duque frowned, and then he saw the heavy imprint of his finger marks upon her arms, and the pallor of her cheeks.

'*Por deus*, Juliet,' he muttered harshly. '*Perdao!* I am sorry!'

Juliet rubbed her arms weakly. 'You – you're not sorry,' she exclaimed, 'unless you're afraid Estelle may see these marks and imagine something entirely different!' Her voice broke.

But she had goaded him too far, for his eyes darkened, and he pulled her to him, his arms sliding round her back, pressing her body close against his, so that she was wholly conscious of the hard strength of his body. Juliet had no strength left with which to fight, even had she wanted to do so, and when his mouth sought and found hers, parting her lips, drawing all resistance out of her, she responded in the way her whole mind and body longed to respond. Her arms slid convulsively round his neck, her fingers tangling in the thick vitality of his hair, and she was no longer conscious of anything or anybody but Felipe, his caressing hands in the small of her back, the passionate heat of his body, and the devastating sensuality of his mouth.

Neither of them were aware of the door opening, and only Teresa's horrified gasp brought them both back to a sensibility of the present. Juliet tore herself out of Felipe's arms, finding the strength somehow in that awful moment. Awful, because as her brain began to function again, she realized just what the Duque had proved with that kiss. He had not kissed her because he wanted to, but because she had goaded him into it, and now he would despise her because she had responded so wantonly to his deliberate expertise. She rubbed her mouth with the back of her hand, hating him and loving him all in one soul-destroying emotion.

The Duke regained his composure almost at once, but Teresa had swung round her chair, and was propelling it furiously away across the hall. Juliet looked at the Duque agonizingly, and then ran out of the room and after Teresa. She heard the study door slam behind her, but glancing back she realized the Duque was still inside.

Teresa's chair sped along the corridor towards her room, but Juliet ran quicker, and she caught her before she could get inside and lock her door.

'Teresa, please,' she begged. 'Wait! Let me explain!'

Teresa's cheeks were stained with tears, and she shook her head dumbly. 'You – you were my friend!' she said chokingly. 'You were my friend!'

Juliet halted the chair by Teresa's door, and opening it, pushed her inside. Then she closed the door again, and went down on her knees beside Teresa's chair.

'Please, please, Teresa,' she said unsteadily. 'Please let me explain.'

Teresa shook her head. 'There's nothing to explain. You're just like the others: like Estelle, and Laura Weston. You don't care about me, you only want Felipe!'

Juliet compressed her lips. 'That's not true, Teresa, and you know it. Of course I care about you. You know I do. The scene you just witnessed between your uncle and myself should never have happened. It was all my fault, I admit, and yet—' She halted. 'Oh, Teresa, it's such a complicated mess. It was all a misunderstanding, that was all.'

Teresa dried her eyes on a handkerchief, and looked down at Juliet stiffly. 'I ought to have known,' she said tautly. 'Felipe is too attractive.'

'Teresa, for God's sake!' Juliet got to her feet. 'Look, honey, I've got to convince you. Your uncle doesn't care a damn about me! I'm not saying he doesn't care about Estelle; I'm sure he does. I'm sure she will get her way and marry him. But I don't want our friendship to be killed by a misunderstanding.'

Teresa looked down at her hands. 'What makes you

so sure he'll marry Estelle?' she asked. 'Has – has he said so?'

'Not in so many words perhaps, but it's there. I know it is. Besides, Estelle has all her plans made. You must know that!'

'Yes. I know what Estelle wants.' Teresa screwed her handkerchief into a ball. 'What about you? What do you want?'

Juliet felt her cheeks burn. 'What do you mean?'

'Felipe warned me not to say anything to you, but that day we were in Barbados, he went back to the Club to find out who it was you were meeting.'

That explained Teresa's uncharacteristic silence on the journey home from Bridgetown.

'Yes, he told me,' Juliet said now.

'He didn't tell me the man's name, but I know he had him investigated. I expect he got the report this morning.'

That explained the delay, thought Juliet wryly.

'I see,' she said, biting her lips. 'Your – your uncle seems to imagine he is a kind of – what we would call in England – sugar-daddy!'

'Sugar-daddy?' Teresa's eyes were wide. 'What is that?'

'Oh, well, it's a kind of older man who – well, takes care of a younger woman.'

'You mean my uncle thinks you are this man's mistress?' Teresa could be staggeringly adult at times.

'Well – yes.'

'And is he?'

'*No!*' Juliet was vehement. 'No, he – he's well, he's a

relation.'

'Did you tell my uncle that?'

'No.' Juliet sighed. 'Oh, heavens, Teresa, this is getting us nowhere. Do you believe me when I say that your uncle was not to blame for this morning's fiasco?'

'I suppose I do.' Teresa bent her head. 'You know I love Felipe. I always will love Felipe.'

Juliet halted in front of her. 'Yes, I know that, Teresa.'

'Does my uncle know?'

'Yes.'

'But he does not love me!' Teresa's eyes were tortured.

'Oh, Teresa, of course he loves you! But not as a man loves the woman who is going to be his wife!' Juliet turned away. 'That's an entirely different thing.'

Teresa was silent for a while and then she said, 'I used to think love was – well, kindness, and tenderness, and affection. That's what love is, to me. When Felipe spoke to me, I felt that warmth and affection. When – when he speaks to you, he doesn't use the same tone. He sometimes seems to hate you—'

'I'm sure he does!' muttered Juliet bitterly, leaning against the window frame.

'I don't think he hates you,' said Teresa, with emphasis. 'I don't think he hates you at all. And today—'

'I've told you – forget what happened today,' exclaimed Juliet, swinging round.

'I can't. Oh, I couldn't forget that? Could you? The way he was holding you – the way he was kissing you! It was – it was – a kind of revelation. I – I don't think I would like it if Felipe treated me like that!'

Juliet stared at her. 'Are you serious?'

Teresa nodded slowly. 'I – I think so. And – and that day when we saw you with that man – that man in Barbados. He was old enough to be your father, much older than Felipe of course, but then you're older than me, and I thought – oh, *senhorita*, I thought, that could be me, in years to come, if I married Felipe. He would be old – and I would still be young!'

Juliet felt an immense sensation of relief overtaking all other emotions suddenly, and momentarily.

'Do you realize what you are saying, Teresa?'

'Of course I realize it.' Teresa looked tremulously up at Juliet. 'In fact, I think I've known it for a very long time. Oh, I was jealous, I still am, a bit, of Felipe spending a long time with somebody else, but I think if I had other friends – other things to do, I could stand it.'

Juliet wanted to laugh and cry all at the same time. If nothing else had come out of this sorry mess, at least Teresa had realized that her feelings towards Felipe could never remain the most important thing in her life. Maybe now those useless limbs would regain the power to be used again.

She stared at the girl, her own emotions spilling over, as tears provided their own relief. Then with an exclamation she went down beside the chair, and hugged Teresa closely.

Teresa looked in surprise at Juliet's tears. 'What is the matter? I thought you'd be pleased,' she said. 'I know Estelle will be.' This last was said with just a trace of bitterness.

At the mention of Estelle's name, Juliet felt her new-found happiness evaporate. Releasing Teresa she rose to her feet again.

'So maybe now we can make real progress with those legs of yours,' she said, with a forcedly light tone.

Teresa was still eyeing her strangely, but she smilingly agreed. Juliet rubbed her eyes dry, and endeavoured to recover her lost composure.

'It – it's getting late,' she said unsteadily. 'I must go and get washed before lunch. Where – where is Francisco?'

Teresa shrugged. 'He left. I don't think Felipe's welcome was particularly enthusiastic, do you? Anyway, he seemed to take the hint. I don't know why Felipe doesn't like him. I always thought he did.'

Juliet shrugged and walked to the door.

'So you'll be all right now?' she said, needing that reassurance.

Teresa nodded. 'Of course. I'll be fine. Just don't expect me to fall over myself with excitement when Felipe and Estelle announce their betrothal.'

Juliet half-smiled, and left the room. Then she made her way swiftly to her room, praying she would encounter nobody on the way. She didn't, and in the seclusion of her room, the forced brightness left her face, and she felt completely haggard.

She walked to the mirror, surveying her drawn features critically. Well, she said to her reflection, what now?

Then she turned away, pressing a hand to her mouth. Teresa was cured, or at least, well on the way to being so. Now, the tables were turned, and she was the loser. And what would the Duque do now? He could dismiss her, of course, although maybe if Teresa wanted her, she would be allowed to stay.

But could she stay? That was more to the point. The Duque despised her for what he thought she was, and without revealing her identity she could not tell him the truth. And if she told him the truth, she would very likely be dismissed out of hand. The Duque would consider she had only taken the job for kicks, to provide a poor little rich girl with some new conversation. He would never believe she wanted the job as desperately as any other girl without employment.

A glance at her watch confirmed that it was almost lunchtime. The thought of food nauseated her, and yet she must pretend, to Teresa at least, that everything was going to go on as before.

She washed, cleaned her teeth, combed order back into hair mussed by the Duque's urgent, compelling fingers, and descended the staircase.

CHAPTER NINE

THERE was a guest for lunch, Estelle Vinceiro.

Juliet seated herself, hoping no one would take any notice of her. The Duque, apart from glancing once in her direction, ignored her, and Teresa seemed to be aware that Juliet did not want irresponsible chatter.

Juliet picked at her meal, endeavouring to eat a little to fill the empty void of her stomach, and became conscious of the fact that Senhora Vinceiro's gaze was frequently cast in her direction, with a strange malevolence in its depth.

Juliet couldn't understand why Estelle should look at her so strangely, unless – her heart somersaulted at the thought – unless the Duque had amused himself by telling Estelle of their contretemps that morning. She felt the blood drain out of her cheeks at the thought. Surely even the Duque could not be so cruel. And yet she had had an example of his cruelty this morning, and she had been forced to wear a light cardigan over her dress to hide the tell-tale bruises the Duque's hard fingers had inflicted.

But to imagine him telling Estelle how she, Juliet, had practically thrown herself at his head, allowing him to kiss her in a way that no decent Portuguese woman would allow, was a destroying thought. And yet for what other reason could Estelle have grown to despise her, and it was contempt that she read in Estelle's eyes.

When the meal was over and Teresa had gone for her rest, accompanied by a rather smug-looking Nurse Madison, the Duque excused himself to Estelle and left the room, a few minutes later disappearing in the direction of the stables. Juliet, engrossed with her own thoughts, had hardly been aware of the others leaving, and when she realized she was alone with Estelle she rose too, eager to escape the older woman's prying eyes.

But Estelle walked to the dining-room door, and closed it, leaning back against it, preventing Juliet's escape. Juliet looked in the direction of the french doors on to the terrace, but Estelle shook her head.

'There is nowhere you can hide on Venterra that I will not eventually find you, Senhorita Summers,' she said, slowly and coldly. 'There are things to be said between us that must be said, and afterwards you will be at liberty to leave not only the *quinta* but the island!'

Juliet felt very tired. It had been a tiring day, and she felt rather like a marathon runner must feel after a particularly gruelling race.

'What is it, *senhora*?' she asked wearily. 'I am very tired. The heat. . . .' She allowed the sentence to melt into the air.

Estelle's delicate features were contorted. 'How dare you stand there, *senhorita*, asking me why I want to speak to you! You know exactly why I want to speak to you! Did you imagine your foolishness with the Duque would remain confidential?' she sneered as Juliet whitened. 'Poor Rosemary! Did you really imagine Felipe would keep such an amusing, pitiful experience to himself?'

Juliet sank down on to a chair, pressing the palms of her hands against her cheeks.

'You mean he has told you?' she said exhaustedly.

'Naturally! Good lord, I am his fiancée, or had you forgotten? Maybe you hoped he had forgotten also!' Estelle paced towards her, surveying her without compassion. 'I believe I once warned you, *senhorita*, Felipe is very attractive. And I suppose as a man he has all the normal reactions to promiscuity!'

'I am not promiscuous!' exclaimed Juliet.

'Then what would you call it? Oh, I admit, you've been rather cleverer than Laura Weston, and your method of attack has been more subtle, but fundamentally you both suffer from the same delusions! Winning Teresa's confidence, and ultimately her friendship, was particularly brilliant. I hardly believed anyone could do that. But now I hear that Teresa has even realized the futility of loving a man like Felipe, a man moreover who is far too old for her. You've done your job well. I suppose I ought to thank you. You, at least, have paved the sure way to my marriage to Felipe.'

Juliet stared at her. 'How do you know about Teresa – and – and the Duque?'

Estelle shrugged. 'Your conversation with Teresa took place in Teresa's sitting-room, did it not? Did you not wonder where Nurse Madison might be?'

'You mean she eavesdropped?' Juliet felt slightly

sickened.

'Yes. She was in the bedroom. She and I have never been what you would call – er – friends. However, she does have one weakness – money! When it became apparent that your friendship with Teresa was undermining her position here, she was quite willing to perform small services for me for a consideration!'

'Oh, you're despicable!' exclaimed Juliet, shaking her head. 'How can you cheat and connive without any thought for anyone but yourself? I don't believe you love Felipe! All you want is to be mistress of the *quinta*!'

Estelle gave a light laugh. 'Love! What is love? I doubt very much whether you know, Senhorita Summers. If you mean the romantic attachment of the male for the female, then that can swiftly be assuaged by physical union!'

Juliet got to her feet on legs that felt like jelly. 'You're mistaking sex for love,' she exclaimed harshly. 'Oh, sex comes into it, but love is not something to be tossed about so lightly, to be laughed about. Love is a destructive powerful force, more powerful than you'll ever know!' Her eyes were bright with unshed tears. She would not break down before this cold, unfeeling, selfish woman.

But Estelle did not notice. Instead she said: 'It seems I was right though, *senhorita*, doesn't it? You do imagine yourself in love with the Duque!'

Juliet clenched her fists. 'My feelings are nothing to do with you – or the Duque! My job was – *is* to care for Teresa!'

'And you intend to carry on with it now, knowing that the Duque is aware of your adolescent passion for him?' Estelle was mocking.

Juliet stiffened. Until Estelle actually voiced the words, the whole pathetic state of her position had remained in embryo. Now, with those few words, she had created a picture of Juliet's life here, if she continued as Teresa's companion. She would be living constantly in the shadow of her own humiliation, and even the prospect of her father's domination seemed paltry by comparison.

Estelle seemed to sense her thoughts, for she said: 'Poor little Rosemary! You've succeeded in curing Teresa, only to catch the disease yourself!'

Juliet shook her head blindly, unable to speak coherently. Estelle had moved away from the door, and she brushed past the older woman, throwing open the door and hastening up the stairs to her room. Once there the tears would not be checked, and all the misery she had experienced that day enveloped her in its shadow.

But she was not by nature a self-pitying girl, and soon she dried her eyes, and sitting down on the edge of her bed, she began to think seriously of leaving. To run away was an admission of defeat, but it didn't seem to matter any more.

Teresa, her first and most important responsibility, no longer really needed her. She had restored the girl's confidence, all that was needed now was time and patience, two qualities any nurse must possess. Even Nurse Madison could no longer prevent the inevitable.

Teresa had a taste for life, for youthfulness, again. She would be all right.

The Duque; well, the Duque would be glad to be rid of her. By staying she would cause him unnecessary embarrassment, and besides, her own self-respect would not allow her to stay knowing with what amusement he regarded her. What disturbed her most about him was his innate sense of duty, and he might insist that she had applied for this position, and that therefore she should offer some concrete explanation for her abrupt departure.

That being so, there was only one solution left to her. She must leave without his knowledge. She had no doubt if she appealed to Estelle Vinceiro for help she would get it, but she had no wish to have any further dealings with her.

No! This was something she must do alone. She chewed desperately at her lower lip. But how? She could hardly order the hydroplane without the Duque's knowledge, and their isolation here did not aid any attempts at a secret departure.

Then a thought struck her. The day, that first disturbing day, when the Duque had taken herself and Teresa to Lauganca Bay he had stopped in the village to see about supplies which were coming in on the island steamer. She remembered then that Consuelo had mentioned the island steamer, telling her that it was the way the islanders visited St. Lucia and St. Vincent. If *she* could take this island steamer, she could easily pick up a charter flight from either of the larger islands. Money was no problem. Even in the Caribbean, the name of Robert Lindsay carried plenty of weight. Once back in London, she could write at length to Teresa, explaining her actions, and possibly asking her to visit her there. After all, she had grown quite fond of Teresa, and through her she would at least hear a little about the Duque, even if such news would be bitter-sweet.

But the island steamer only visited the island twice weekly, and tomorrow was one of those days. That gave her little time to plan any kind of subterfuge. She sighed. Was it really only five or six weeks ago that she had been planning her escape from London, only now to find herself planning an almost identical journey home? Rosemary would think she was completely crazy, and her father – well, her father would feel very pleased that he had won, even if only indirectly.

When the time for evening dinner came round, she sent a message with one of the maids, excusing herself on the pretext that she had a headache. The ache in her head was real enough, but actually she needed time to think, and to pack, and she had no desire to meet the Duque again before her departure. Those piercing dark eyes might penetrate her inmost thoughts and discover the guilty plans she was making.

It would be impossible, of course, to take all her luggage. An overnight change of clothes thrust into her basket-bag would have to suffice. When she left the *quinta* the following afternoon she wanted no one to suspect that she was bent on anything but a shopping expedition. Such a pastime was not unknown to her, and Miguel would get a car for her as he always did, without any reason for suspecting her destination.

As though to aid her plans, the next morning, the Duque did not appear at breakfast. Teresa explained that during the night there had been a fire in the cane fields, and although the fire had been extinguished, the Duque would be out all day inspecting the damage.

She studied Juliet's pale cheeks with some anxiety, seeing the dark rings that sleeplessness had circled round her eyes.

'What's wrong?' she asked, frowning. 'Are you anxious about what happened yesterday? I'm sure you have no reason to be.'

Juliet wondered on what she based the essence of that remark. 'It's nothing,' she denied, attempting a light tone. 'I admit I slept badly, but that's all. I – well, I haven't felt too well this morning. I thought perhaps we might spend a lazy day. I think I'll adopt the habit of siesta in the afternoons, too.' She managed a short laugh.

Teresa was not convinced, but forbore to say any more, respecting Juliet's silence. Juliet was glad. She couldn't have borne a long argument about her health. It would improve, once she had got the Duque de Castro out of her system.

Only the certain knowledge that she would never get the Duque de Castro out of her system mocked her tremulous thoughts.

After lunch, she pretended to be going to take the siesta as she had told Teresa, but after the young girl was settled in her room, Juliet came back downstairs, carrying her basket-bag and handbag, dressed casually enough in slim-fitting dark blue pants and a loose white overblouse. The jacket that matched the pants was over her arm. It might be considerably cooler when she landed in London.

Miguel brought out the shooting brake for her, smiling at her in his usual admiring way. He looked up at the sun, and said:

'It's a very hot day, *senhorita*. Do not stay out in the sun too long.'

Juliet smiled politely, and nodded. 'Thanks, Miguel. I won't,' and then she drove away, her legs quaking in fear of being stopped at the last moment.

But why should any one stop her? No one knew her plans except herself. Certainly she had done nothing unusual in taking out the car. Her greatest difficulty would be boarding the island steamer without attracting attention to herself.

The quay at Venterra was crowded, the steamer already loaded and only awaiting its final departure forms. Juliet hurried up the gangplank, meeting the dark-skinned Captain at its top.

'*Senhorita*,' he murmured politely, recognizing her as the new companion to the ward of the Duque by the colour of her auburn hair. 'Can I be of assistance?'

His old-world politeness almost overwhelmed Juliet.

'Oh, yes, please,' she said glancing round nervously. 'Could – could we go somewhere and speak privately?'

The Captain frowned, then nodded, and summoned his second in command to take over. 'Come,' he said.

'We will go to my cabin.'

In the Captain's cabin Juliet said, as briefly as possible, that she wished for transportation to St. Lucia.

The Captain frowned. 'But why are you not using the Duque's hydroplane?' he questioned, obviously puzzled and disturbed.

Juliet sighed. 'The Duque and I have had a disagreement,' she said, at last. 'I want to leave, but I do not wish to use any transport owned by the Duque.'

The Captain half-smiled. 'The Duque owns most of this vessel,' he remarked dryly.

Juliet pressed her hands together, and stared at him pleadingly. 'Will you take me with you?' she asked imploringly.

The Captain frowned. If the Duque had had an argument with the girl, why was she not being removed from the island as swiftly as possible in the hydroplane? And where was her luggage? He had no desire to fall foul of his employer, and he was very much afraid this young woman was in more trouble than she cared to admit.

Yet for all that he felt sorry for her. She was such a slender creature, so fair and helpless. How could he ignore the plea in those beseeching eyes? Ignoring the dictates of his brain, he said:

'All right, all right, I will take you, *senhorita*.'

She could have hugged him, she was so pleased. 'Thank you, thank you,' she exclaimed effusively, and the Captain's dark skin darkened even more with embarrassment.

Even as they spoke, Juliet heard the throb of the

engines being started, and the Captain excused himself to negotiate their departure. Juliet remained in the cabin, peering through the porthole with eyes suddenly misty with tears. She had never realized she was such an emotional creature, but apart from the beauty of Venterra, she was leaving behind the only man she could ever love.

The journey to St. Lucia was accomplished by nightfall. Juliet, after the ship had cleared the harbour, had gone up on deck, welcoming the cooling breeze, and the gentle swell of the water. No one troubled her. The other passenger, all dark-skinned islanders, eyed her with some trepidation, and even the Captain kept his distance. In truth, Juliet thought perhaps he was already regretting his impulsive acceptance of herself as a passenger.

They docked at Castries in the early evening. The town twinkled with lights, while Juliet could vaguely distinguish the steep plateau of Morne Fortune rising like a bastion above the harbour. She had never been alone in such a strange, alien place at night before, and she experienced no small misgivings when it was time to disembark.

The Captain seemed concerned about her, too, for he said: 'Do you have anywhere to go, *senhorita*?'

Juliet linked her hands. 'Not – not exactly,' she murmured. 'But I can manage.'

The Captain frowned. 'Are you leaving the island tomorrow?' he asked with some perspicacity.

Juliet nodded. 'I hope to get a charter flight.'

'I see. Well, *senhorita*, I shall be remaining on board tonight, but my cabin is at your disposal if you would care to use it.'

Juliet stared at him. 'You – you would let me do that? Stay here?'

'Of course. Why not? I have children of my own, *senhorita*, and the quayside of Castries is not a suitable place for a young girl alone at night.'

Juliet grasped his hand. 'I'm – I'm very grateful to you. You'll never know how grateful, *senhor*.'

The Captain was embarrassed again, and she said no more. But as she lay later in the evening, watching the winking stars in the sky above, just like some jewelled sapphire velvet, she wondered how she would ever be able to repay him. He had taken no money for her passage, and without his assistance she might have found herself in a very difficult situation. Alone, and without luggage, she was a target for every kind of awkward situation.

Although she had not expected to sleep, the lazy wash of the ship, and her own exhaustion of the night before, overwhelmed her, and to her surprise when she opened her eyes again and glanced at her watch, it was already seven-thirty.

She had not undressed completely, merely removing her pants and blouse, and now she washed in the Captain's little hand basin, cleaned her teeth, and combed her hair. Then she went on deck.

The Captain was sitting at a table, eating rolls and fruit, and he invited her to join him. The coffee was delicious, and although she drank two cups together with a cigarette, she refused his offers of food.

'You can take a taxi to the airport,' said the Captain, obviously determined to assure her safely on her way. 'I myself will get one for you.'

'You've been more than kind,' said Juliet unsteadily. 'I can't thank you enough.'

The Captain shook his head. 'I only hope you know what you are doing,' he murmured, almost inaudibly, but Juliet appreciated his concern.

The airport which served St. Lucia was not large, but Juliet was in luck. She was able to arrange a flight later the same morning. In the meantime she took herself into the small reception lounge to wait.

She smoked several cigarettes, ordered coffee, and waited impatiently, wondering uneasily whether she had been reported as a missing person. If she had, there was really only Teresa to care, one way or the other. How pleased Estelle would be that she had got rid of her so simply! How she and the Duque would laugh about her fugitive departure.

She heard the sound of a powerful car, sweeping up the road to the reception lounge. The tyres screamed in indignation at their rough treatment, as they brought the car to an abrupt halt at the doors to the airport buildings.

Juliet glanced round casually, wondering who could be causing such a disturbance, and saw the two men enter the building together almost as someone in a dream, seeing unreal characters acting out an unreal drama.

Then she rose to her feet, glancing about her desperately, feeling trapped and frightened and exhilarated all in one compelling emotion. Incredibly it was Felipe, and her father!

The Duque strode ahead of the older man, reaching Juliet first, staring at her with tortured eyes, and then suddenly grasping her hand, and turning it palm uppermost, put his mouth to its centre, closing her fingers over the kiss.

'*Deus!*' he muttered heavily. 'If this is what you did to your father, it is no wonder he was anxious about you! If you ever do it to me again – I will kill you!'

And Juliet knew he meant it!

Then Robert Lindsay reached them, looking at Juliet with eyes that were strangely tender, and half amused.

'So,' he said, 'at last we've caught up with you. You're a devil for running away, Juliet. When are you going to stop and realize that you can't run away from life?'

Juliet shook her head, feeling suddenly giddy with fatigue and sheer nervous exhaustion.

'I wasn't running away from life,' she murmured weakly. 'Oh, Dad!' and ignominiously she burst into tears, burying her face on her father's shoulder, as she had done as a child.

Robert Lindsay looked at the Duque over his daughter's shoulder. 'It seems you were right, Felipe,' he said enigmatically.

Juliet gathered herself together, feeling relieved that at least the lounge was deserted. Drying her eyes, she said:

'I don't understand any of this. What's going on? Why are you together? And why have you—' she looked at the Duque '– why have you come after me?'

The Duque glanced at her father, and Robert Lindsay nodded. 'All right, all right,' he said resignedly, 'I'll wait outside.'

He smiled encouragingly at them both, and then walked away, leaving them alone.

Juliet twisted her hands together, avoiding Felipe's eyes. There was some catch to this, there had to be. Why had Felipe come? What had her father told him? What had he told her father?

The Duque gave an angry exclamation, and said: 'Juliet, I know all about your deception. I know you are Lindsay's daughter. It makes not the slightest difference to me.'

Juliet looked up. 'How – I mean – when did you meet my father?'

'Yesterday. After you had left on the steamer. He arrived in a hydroplane, and came straight to see me. We had a very comprehensive conversation, and I think we understand one another completely. It was not until later that you were discovered to be missing!' His pallor could be seen despite the dark tan of his skin. '*Deus!* You cannot imagine how I felt!'

Juliet turned away. His words meant little to her. All right, her father had cleared up the mystery of her relationship to him, and he and the Duque obviously spoke the same language. But that really made no difference to her.

'The – the plane leaves in half an hour,' she said

unsteadily. 'For goodness' sake, if you have a point, make it!'

There was a stifled ejaculation from the Duque, and then she felt him twist her violently round to face him, almost throwing her off balance. 'Damn you, Juliet,' he muttered unevenly, 'do you want me to crawl to you? Because if that is necessary, I will!'

Juliet stared at him tremulously. 'I don't understand,' she exclaimed. 'What do you want me to say?'

But this was too much. With a groan, he gathered her close against him, and once more she felt the passionate pressure of his mouth parting her own. Only this time when his mouth dragged itself away from hers it sought the soft curve of her neck, the smoothness of her ears and cheeks, and the fluttering moistness of her eyes, before burying itself on hers again, destroying any defences she might have tried to sustain.

At last he leaned his forehead against hers, and she could feel his body trembling when she slid her arms round him, wriggling inside his jacket against the hard warmth that she, incredibly, had the power to arouse.

'Does that make it a little plainer?' he muttered, a trifle thickly. 'It is as well your good father is outside, for I am only human and I confess I want you very badly.'

Juliet blushed becomingly, drawing back a little.

'But Estelle—' she began, shaking her head.

'Estelle means no more to me today than she did ten years ago when she married my cousin,' said Felipe firmly. 'Any ideas she might have had were purely illusions.'

Juliet sighed. 'But you never gave me any indication,' she exclaimed. 'I thought I was a nuisance!'

Felipe half-smiled. 'You were – you are – but a nuisance I personally cannot live without. *Pequena*, I adore you.'

'Felipe!' she gasped, only slightly delaying his kiss. 'Tell me about this. I want to know. When did you find me – well, attractive?'

He smiled charmingly. 'When did I find you attractive?' he repeated lazily. 'Well, I suppose I found you attractive, right from the start, right from the moment you stood so slim and scared on the staircase of the *quinta*. As to when I fell in love with you – that took a little longer. Two days, to be precise. Two days in which my whole world was shattered. I couldn't believe it. I had to go away on business, and I stayed away, endeavouring to rid myself of this painful affliction that was disturbing my sleep. But it was no good. When I came back, it was worse than ever. When I saw you with Francisco Valmos I could have killed him.' He smiled. 'I think I must have had some very violent ancestors. I find my emotions almost uncontrollable where you are concerned.' He kissed the nape of her neck, twisting her hair round his fingers. 'I wanted to tell you, but you always seemed to be avoiding me. Whenever our hands or bodies touched, you, flinched. I was afraid you did not like me very much, and I was afraid I might scare you away. Then when you met – your father, that day in Barbados, I wanted to kill you, too. I hated you, believe me. Because I thought you were not the person I believed you to be, the woman I loved to distraction. When I found out who he was, I was incensed. The idea that you might be his daughter never even entered my head. Why should it? You had never hinted at such a thing, even though now I recall little things, like your driving through the Alps, and the awful mess you made of pretending you didn't know how to skin-dive.'

Juliet allowed herself a small chuckle. It was such a marvellous, marvellous day!

'Go on,' she said, and he laughed.

'You are vain, Juliet,' he said, frowning. 'You want me to abase myself.'

'Entirely,' she answered mischievously. 'I thought you were so arrogant, so cold, so cruel!'

'Cruel, maybe,' he agreed, sighing. 'That day in my study I wanted to hurt you, but when I had done so, I was horrified. When I kissed you, I began to believe you cared for me too, and then Teresa interrupted us, and you fled away as though you despised me, and I despised myself for doing what I had always planned not to do – frighten you!'

'You only frightened me because I loved you so much,' whispered Juliet weakly.

'Is that so? Is that really so?' He gathered her closer. 'Finally, yesterday, when I discovered you had gone, just when my anxieties about Robert Lindsay had been dispersed, I was almost out of my mind. Estelle can be in no doubt as to my feelings for you. Our last meeting was anything but friendly. I do not think she will stay long on Venterra.'

'Wait, though,' said Juliet suddenly. 'Did you – did you discuss our – our embrace in your study with her?'

'No!' He swore softly. '*Deus!* What do you think I am?'

Juliet shook her head. 'It must have been Nurse Madison. Why didn't I think of that? Of course!'

'Yes, they must both leave,' said the Duque, his voice suddenly cold, and Juliet shivered a little. 'Nurse Madison has attempted to ingratiate herself once too often. Besides, Teresa tells me she feels confident she will walk again in time. She seems to get along incredibly well with your father. In fact, I think you may find that your father will take Teresa away with him when he returns to England, after our marriage.'

'Our marriage?' echoed Juliet, in astonishment.

The Duque smiled down at her, his eyes tender. 'Of course. Did you think I could wait much longer?'

Juliet buried her face against his chest. 'Did I say I wanted to wait?' she murmured, and the Duque gave a lazy, triumphant laugh, as his mouth sought hers again.

Then there was an apologetic cough, and Juliet turned in the Duque's arms to see her father leaning against the door jamb.

'I don't like to be an intruder,' he remarked, smiling, 'but after combing every hotel in St. Lucia, not to mention the waterfront, I could do with a drink, and I don't mean coffee!'

Juliet looked up at Felipe. 'I feel intoxicated

already,' she said unsteadily, and Felipe, putting an arm across her shoulders led her across to her father.

'I take it you will be staying for the wedding,' he remarked, smiling.

Robert Lindsay frowned. 'Tell me,' he said, 'is there a stock exchange in St. Lucia?' and Juliet linked her arm with his, laughing merrily.

FREE!
Romance Treasury

**A beautifully bound,
value-packed,
three-in-one
volume of romance!**

FREE!

A hardcover Romance Treasury volume
containing 3 treasured works of romance
by 3 outstanding Harlequin authors...

...as your introduction to Harlequin's
Romance Treasury subscription plan!

Romance Treasury

...almost 600 pages of exciting romance reading
every month at the low cost of $6.97 a volume!

A wonderful way to collect many of Harlequin's most beautiful love
stories, all originally published in the late '60s and early '70s.
Each value-packed volume, bound in a distinctive gold-embossed
leatherette case and wrapped in a colorfully illustrated dust jacket,
contains...
- 3 full-length novels by 3 world-famous authors of romance fiction
- a unique illustration for every novel
- the elegant touch of a delicate bound-in ribbon bookmark...
  and much, much more!

Romance Treasury

...for a library of romance you'll treasure forever!

Complete and mail today the FREE gift certificate and subscription
reservation on the following page.

Romance Treasury

An exciting opportunity to collect treasured works of romance! Almost 600 pages of exciting romance reading in each beautifully bound hardcover volume!

You may cancel your subscription whenever you wish! You don't have to buy any minimum number of volumes. Whenever you decide to stop your subscription just drop us a line and we'll cancel all further shipments.

FREE!
Romance Treasury

Three beautiful love stories
...in one elegant volume!

See coupon on facing page.

Escape! Juliet savored the word

For years, Juliet's father had used his wealth, power and influence to rule her life. But now, she was free to make her own decisions. She had assumed a new name and identity, and had run away to a job on this beautiful West Indian island.

But had she jumped from the frying pan into the fire?

Bad as her father had been, her employer, the Duque Felipe Ricardo de Castro, turned out to be even more domineering. And what was worse—Juliet fell in love with him!

 Harlequin Books

The most popular romance fiction all over the world... because no one touches the heart of a woman quite like Harlequin!